Red Fox Road

RED FOX ROAD

Frances Greenslade

PUFFIN CANADA

an imprint of Penguin Random House Canada Young Readers,
a Penguin Random House Company

Published in hardcover by Puffin Canada, 2020

1 2 3 4 5 6 7 8 9 10

Manufactured in Canada

Library and Archives Canada Cataloguing in Publication

Title: Red Fox Road / Frances Greenslade.
Names: Greenslade, Frances, 1961- author.
Identifiers: Canadiana (print) 20190188553 | Canadiana (ebook)
20190188561 | ISBN 9780735267817 (hardcover) |
ISBN 9780735267824 (EPUB)
Classification: LCC PS8613.R438 R43 2020 | DDC jC813/.6—dc23

Library of Congress Control Number: 2019950435

www.penguinrandomhouse.ca

Penguin
Random House
PUFFIN CANADA

To my sister Barbie,
who always says yes to adventures.

CHAPTER ONE

Mom wasn't speaking to Dad, but Dad hadn't noticed. His eyebrows, which I could see in the rearview mirror, plowed toward his nose in his worried look, but he probably hadn't noticed that either. When Dad drove, his focus was total. And this road required more focus than most. Sharp rocks pocked the hard-packed mud, and rivulets of rain had snaked across the surface, carving ruts like small valleys. Dad braked and checked his route, the front tires plunged down, the truck rocked crazily and Mom braced herself against the dashboard. Then we climbed out of the rut again and barely missed a rock the size of a microwave.

All this with not a word out of Dad. Mom once told us that when she drove she could zone out for miles and suddenly come to, wondering where she was and how she'd gotten there. She had asked Dad what he thought about when he drove.

"Driving," he said.

The funny thing was that it wasn't a joke. Mom said Dad was the safest driver she knew and she trusted him completely. She wasn't saying that now.

About two hours and fifty miles ago (I checked the odometer and, yes, it took us that long to cover fifty miles), they'd had a fight. It was the first day of our trip to the Grand Canyon. Dad wanted to take this shortcut because we'd made a wrong turn and not noticed for nearly two hours. We'd stopped for gas in a small town, and then come out of the gas station and somehow ended up on the wrong highway.

I was the one who noticed that we were heading west, not south, but by then we'd gone miles out of our way. Dad's new GPS showed this road that would save us a little over a hundred miles of backtracking. The shortcut on the GPS was a thin line that joined up with a bigger line, a highway south of here. Once we got there, we'd have to make two turns to get back on the route we'd started on. But Mom didn't trust the GPS. She had the paper map of Oregon spread on her lap. The map had a slogan on the cover: *We Love Dreamers*. I liked that, and it made me a little bit on Mom's side. Of the two, Mom was more the dreamer than Dad, a fact I'd just realized. The line Dad wanted to follow wasn't on the map. It wasn't like him to go off the beaten path, which made me think he was pretty sure about the road.

"It's a logging road, Del," Dad had said. "Logging roads don't show up on road maps."

"Some do," Mom said. "Anyway, what makes you think it's a logging road? There's no sign."

"It's obvious. We're in the middle of a forest in Oregon—it has to be a logging road."

"I don't know why you're so eager to go on this wild adventure today of all days, when it's all I can do to get you out of the house most of the time. It's been a long day already. I'd just like to get to the motel before dark."

"It's not a wild adventure," Dad said, and he let the other comment pass. "You have to trust the technology."

"Well, I don't," Mom said. "And I don't think it was a great idea to bring that thing along to use for the first time in a totally unfamiliar wilderness."

"It's not a wilderness, it's a logging road."

And then there was the long, angry silence, which Dad hadn't noticed.

As fights go, it wasn't much. I've seen worse between some of my friends' parents, and they don't even care who's listening. Mom and Dad were more the type to let silence do their talking.

This time, I was mostly on Dad's side, because I was the one in the family who liked adventure, and it was true that Dad didn't have the heart for adventures most of the time. When Mom was in a good mood, she said it was because he worked so hard and walked so many miles in his job as a mail carrier that when he wasn't working he just wanted to rest his legs. When she was in what she called "a mood," she said Dad used to be a lot more fun and that he was getting old before his time.

I had my survival guidebook open in my lap, though it was too bumpy to read now. The book was old and dog-eared, with coffee stains on the cover. I'd bought it at a garage sale for twenty-five cents. The compact, wiry man who sold it to me, a man everyone just called Howie, was famous for writing a book about climbing in the bluffs outside our town. As he took my

3

quarter for the book, his eyes twinkled and his eyebrows danced above them like gray caterpillars.

"Going on some adventures?" he said. The anticipation in his voice told me he'd been on many himself.

"I hope so," I said.

"This book is a classic. Take it out to the woods. Practice a little."

That was my plan. I had it open to the page about trapping small animals. I wouldn't be able to practice that where we were going, but I liked to imagine it anyway.

I gazed into the woods now, inviting, mysterious. If we had time, we could stop and explore. But in case you hadn't noticed, adults are always in a hurry. They drive by most of the best stuff in a big rush to get somewhere else—in our case, the motel. So I was glad to be taking our little truck off the main road, bumping over the rocks into this forest where we couldn't see far ahead of us and each curve in the road opened onto something new.

But even I could see that the way the road was deteriorating, it would be hard for big logging trucks to get through here, and if it had once been for logging, it probably wasn't used anymore. Dad must have been thinking that too. But he wasn't saying anything.

The road at first had been bumpy washboard, wide and sunny, with enough room for two vehicles to pass. Scrub alders and a few small firs stretched on either side of the road, bordered by some wild roses, not yet in bloom. Snow had begun to soften into melting, but the sides of the road still held pockets of it, glistening in the sun. It was only April, still cool enough for our hike in the Grand Canyon.

The Grand Canyon was my idea. I never imagined we would actually get to do it. Mom and Dad had surprised me with a card for my thirteenth birthday, which was last month. The card had a picture from a magazine glued to the front, of three people standing on a rock outcropping overlooking mile after mile of folded, red-earthed canyon glowing in the light. Mom had labeled the three people: Mom, Dad and Francie.

Now the road had narrowed. There was only room enough for one vehicle. The woods had changed, too. Huge firs and cedars rose on both sides of the road, their branches dipping into our path in places. The sunlight was mostly blocked out, just winking through feathery cedar fronds in a pretty pattern. I loved the deep-scarred bark of the Douglas firs, like the skin of a very old person's face. I rolled the window down; the perfume of cedar and damp earth drifted in. If I wore perfume, which I didn't, it would have to smell like this.

Mom wiped her hands on her jeans. Her hands get sweaty when she's nervous; we always teased her about it, but I didn't think it was a good idea to tease her now.

Neither Mom nor Dad was saying anything, but it wasn't the kind of comfortable silence we usually had in the truck on our long drives where Mom might suddenly read out a crossword clue she'd been trying to solve for half an hour. It was the kind of silence where Mom was trying not to blow her top, as she called it, because if she said one word, it would be like blowing a radiator hose, which I had seen once—all that hot steam and water comes rushing out and there's nothing you can do to stop it.

I daydreamed about the kind of tree forts I could build in these woods. It looked to me like it wouldn't be that hard to find a frame of crisscrossing branches to use as a platform, and if I had my ax, which I didn't, I could chop up some of that deadfall to build the platform. Dad said we wouldn't need the ax on the Grand Canyon hike. I had no nails, either, of course. The thing about a Grand Canyon hike is that you want your pack as light as possible.

You descend about a vertical mile into the canyon from the rim, or so the website says. That's the easy part. The hard part comes when you have to climb back out. I'd trained by climbing the bleachers at school with my pack on, loaded with a bunch of binders and books. Sometimes Mom joined me, but not always. Even though she's the guidance counselor at the school, so it's easy for her to meet me, after school tends to be her busiest time.

We each had light summer sleeping bags and just the clothes we'd need—one long-sleeved shirt, two T-shirts, one pair of pants, one pair of shorts, a spare pair of socks, underwear, a warm jacket and rain gear. Dad had the tent, and he'd bought a plastic cube to fill in case we needed to carry water between camps. Mom had the stove fuel and first aid kit. I would carry the one-burner stove and one pot to boil water. My pack weighed twenty pounds—we'd taken turns trying them on the bathroom scale at home. But we still needed to add our food. We hadn't been able to find the dehydrated kind in Penticton, and Mom hadn't had time to go to Vancouver or Kelowna to look for it. Our plan was to spend a night in a motel close to the canyon, buy the dehydrated meals, some chocolate, and some fruit, and finish packing. Mom said my pack shouldn't weigh more than twenty pounds, since I only weigh eighty-five pounds "soaking wet," as Dad says. But I wanted to carry my share of the food to prove I could survive out there on my own if I ever needed to.

I didn't need my ax because fires aren't allowed in the canyon anyway. But if you camped in this forest, an ax would be pretty handy to have. Maybe not essential. Essential would be a tent, matches, knife, first aid kit, flashlight, map, compass, extra clothes, food and water. I'd brought my compass on this trip, even though Dad said we were just walking down a well-marked trail and back out again, so there was no chance of getting lost. Also, he had his new handheld GPS, which he wanted to try out.

❖

I must have fallen asleep. A sudden bang that I felt under my seat woke me up.

"That didn't sound good," Mom said.

The truck had bottomed out in a gully. I watched Dad's eyes in the rearview mirror. He blinked, but no more. He gave the truck gas and we banged again, the noise coming from farther back this time, then we climbed out to more level ground.

We drove for another fifteen or twenty minutes. Then Mom said, "Do you think we should turn back?" Her voice was gentler now.

"I don't think we have enough gas to make it back that way," Dad said.

"Have a drink of water," said Mom, passing him the bottle. "Let's stop for a few minutes, take a breather."

"It shouldn't be far now."

We may have gone another five minutes, slowly crawling along the worsening road, when Dad said, "Hmm."

"What is it?" Mom said.

"I think we're overheating a bit."

"Since when?"

"I don't know. I just noticed it."

"Let's stop. Let the engine cool. We've got some bread and cheese. I'm starving."

Dad slowed, put the truck into park and turned it off.

"I don't think we need to pull over out of traffic," he said and winked at me.

We got out. Sweet forest air welcomed us. Moss-covered rocks and fallen trees of every shade of green, lime to deep emerald, covered the forest floor. Ferns and young trees with soft dainty branches like green lace formed the next layer, then the hemlocks with their slender, drooping limbs, hanging with black lichen, and above it all, the firs with deep-fissured bark. I had learned about forests in social studies. Ms. Fineday had taken us out into the woods and had us identify the species by making pencil drawings of them. I had my sketchbook in the truck and was still trying to decide if it was worth the extra weight in my pack to bring it on the hike.

Ms. Fineday had been a forest firefighter before she became a teacher, so she knew the names of every tree this side of the Rockies. She said most people were content to call everything that had needles a pine tree, but that was missing out on the story of the forest. Every forest had a story, she said, and if you could read that story, you could not only appreciate it more but also survive there, if you had to.

"And that knowledge could come in handy. If the zombies come," she said. She only said that to wake up the students who weren't paying attention. But I was always paying attention.

"Can I go explore?" I asked Mom and Dad.

"Don't go out of sight," Dad said.

"I just want to see what's over that ridge."

"Don't go out of sight," Mom repeated. "I'll get out something to eat."

In among the tall firs, the sun warmed patches of vibrant green moss. It looked soft enough to sleep on. Some of the trees had branches covered in moss all the way up, like furry spider legs. I stepped over deadfall. Standing dead trees would make homes for owls, Ms. Fineday told us.

At the base of the ridge, a boulder the size of a car had a small tree growing out of it. I scrambled up its side and looked out over the forest. The sun streamed through the trees. A woodpecker drummed a trunk somewhere nearby. Bands of green rolled out as far as I could see to the north and south, and to the west Mom and Dad stood on the ribbon of dusty road and waved at me.

I reached for a tree root and pulled myself up the rest of the way to the top of the ridge. Beyond it, to the east, more forest, the inviting carpet of moss and another ridge. I would need my hiking boots, a walking stick in case I had to ford any creeks, my jackknife . . . Mom was calling my name. When I turned, I saw that I had walked out of sight of them. I picked up a perfect stick, freshly broken with a knot at one end for a handle. I cracked it against a log to test its strength. Then I climbed back down the ridge and waved at Mom and Dad.

They were sitting in the sun on the tailgate of the truck when I got back. Mom handed me a cheese sandwich.

"Pretty here," she said. She looked up from the map she'd been studying.

"Perfect day," Dad said. The road stretched out behind us, and above it, white balls of cloud billowed on the horizon, with clear blue sky above.

"What would you call that blue?" Dad said.

"Sky blue," said Mom.

"It's not robin's egg," he said.

"It's not turquoise," I said. "Is it azure?" *Azure* was a word I'd learned recently.

"It might be azure. I don't really know what azure looks like," Dad said.

"It's sky blue," said Mom.

"I think it's bluer than that," Dad said.

"The wild blue yonder. I was just noticing how many places in this part of Oregon are called 'wildernesses.' Right up your alley." She jumped down from the tailgate and tapped my head with the folded map.

"Yep," said Dad. "We should get a move on."

I scrambled into the back cab seat, the little seat behind Mom's that faced sideways. It wasn't comfortable, but I rested my feet on the gear that was piled on the floor and that made it a bit better. Grandpa had offered to let us take his SUV, which would have been more comfortable, but Dad said the Mazda was cheaper on gas, since it was only four-cylinder. And we couldn't have come down this road in Grandpa's vehicle.

Dad turned the key. The truck made a clunk-clunk noise and

didn't start. Mom and Dad looked at each other. He tried it again. The same tight clunk and the engine didn't even turn over.

"What's wrong with it?" Mom said. Her voice sounded dry, tight.

Dad didn't answer. He pulled the hood latch and got out. We watched him through the crack as he reached for the oil dipstick, pulled it out and looked at it. He closed the hood and went around to the side of the truck to look under it.

I saw him stand, brush off his jeans and look up the road. I don't think Mom saw that.

He came back and reached under his seat, pulled out the crowbar he kept there. Then he went to the back and tapped on something.

He got back in and tried to start it again. The same dull clunk. He turned to Mom.

"It looks like we might have a hole in the oil pan."

"Can you fix it?" That was probably a sign of the faith that Mom had in Dad. But I knew something she didn't, because I spent Saturdays in the garage with Dad when he worked on our cars that had broken down. I brought him coffee after supper when it was getting dark and chilly out and he had the work light rigged up to shine on whatever engine part he was working on. I liked the smell of oil, and the WD-40 he used to clean bolts. I knew how to test a spark plug gap and trace and cut a new gasket, how to take a tire off if the nut was stuck. And I knew that if we had a hole in the oil pan, that sound we heard when Dad turned the key meant the engine was seized and plugging the hole in the oil pan wouldn't help. We would not be driving out on this logging road. We would not be driving anywhere.

CHAPTER TWO

"We can't fix it, Del," Dad said. "We're in a bit of a situation here."

"A situation?" Mom's voice rose. "You mean we're stranded here in the middle of nowhere."

"I'll have to walk out to the main road. It's not that far."

"You can't walk out. You have no idea where you're going."

"I've got the GPS. I can see the road, Del."

"The GPS got us into this 'situation,' as you call it, in the first place."

I wasn't scared, exactly. But I didn't like that Mom was mad at Dad, that now it seemed as if she'd been right and he shouldn't have taken the back road into the wilderness. It seemed to me that Mom was usually right, in that brutally practical way she had, but I couldn't help myself from taking Dad's side most of the time anyway. Something made me want to stick up for him, and made me wish she wouldn't point out the mistakes he made.

I know you're not supposed to love one of your parents better than the other. Then again, you're not supposed to love one of your children better than the other either.

Dad was looking under the truck again, as if he might see something different than he'd seen the first time. I went and joined him. The road and the rocks were stained dirty brown.

"Yup. As I suspected," Dad said.

"Is the engine seized?"

"I'd say so. It must have been that rock we hit a while back when we bottomed out. We must have been losing oil ever since."

Dad and I both looked down the road, in the direction we were going. It looked less like a road and more like a washed-out trail, scarred with deep runnels where rain had cut into it. A tumble of jagged rocks had collected in the dips. About fifty feet ahead, trees swallowed the road as it curved out of sight.

"I think we're close. This should join up with the highway up there. It shouldn't take me long to cover it."

"You're going to walk?"

"If there's one thing I'm good at, it's walking," he said, smiling at me.

Mom got out of the truck. "I think we should just wait for help," she said. "If we had a cell phone . . ."

"A cell phone wouldn't work out here, even if we did have one," Dad said. "And I think we could wait a long time for someone to come down here."

"I thought you said it was a logging road. It's used all the time."

"I may have been wrong about that."

"Wait until tomorrow at least. We can make a fire. Maybe someone will spot it."

Dad cleared his throat and spat in the dust. He spoke quietly. "No one's going to take any notice of a fire in the middle of the Oregon bush."

They must have both been thinking what I was thinking: that no one would know we were here, and no one would even worry about us for probably a good two weeks. We had not taken the most direct route, either, even before we took the shortcut. Dad said we'd take the faster route back after the hike, when we'd be eager to get home. But for the drive down we'd go into what he called "more interesting country," through the forests of Oregon. That didn't sound like him; except when I thought about it more, it seemed to me he was stalling. He'd rather be driving than hiking. Dad really wasn't an outdoorsy guy. His idea of adventure, Mom said, was taking a Sunday drive.

"We've got everything we need to camp," I said. "I can set up the tent."

"Everything except food," said Mom.

"We've got food," I said. "We've got some, anyway."

"Don't worry," Dad said. He turned to untie the ropes on the tarp covering our gear. "I'll walk out of here tomorrow. I'll start at first light."

I climbed onto the back of the truck with a strange feeling of excitement bubbling in my chest. I should have been afraid, but I'd often imagined how I'd survive if I got stranded in the bush, and now here we were. It was only for a night, but still. It was a chance to practice. I pulled out the tent. It was a small lightweight one for backpacking and was really better suited for two people than three, but I'd convinced Mom and Dad that it would be big enough for our Grand Canyon trip. The website said you could sleep outside under the stars, and that was my plan.

"Where should we set up?"

Mom and Dad both looked into the woods, but they seemed not to have really heard my question. I jumped down and took the tent into a clearing that was just a few feet off the road.

"I'd rather be on the road," Mom said. "If someone comes down here, I don't want to miss them."

"It's too rocky, though."

She looked at the tent distractedly and said, "Put it where you want then."

Dad went off to hike farther up the road to see what condition it was in. I set the tent up easily myself, and rolled our sleeping bags out inside it—Dad's on the outside, Mom's in the middle, mine beside hers. Then I went to gather wood. When I got back with the first armload of branches, Mom was sitting on the tailgate, rolling a cigarette from her secret tobacco pouch.

"I thought you quit," I said.

"I did quit."

"But you brought your pouch."

"It's just in case."

"In case of what?"

"Emergencies." She had her head down and was rolling carefully. She ran her tongue delicately along the edge of the cigarette paper, then met my eyes. "Don't look at me like that."

"Like what?"

"Like you know what."

"This isn't an emergency."

"It's not?" She struck a match and it flared on the end of the cigarette, the skunk-sweet smell of her special tobacco scenting the air.

"It's an adventure," I said.

"Okay, Francie. You have your idea of an adventure and I have my idea of an emergency. Can we agree on that?"

"Can I use your matches? I want to light the fire."

"It's not too early?"

"I'll gather lots of wood. It'll be better with a fire. I'll make you a seat beside it."

She handed them to me, then closed her eyes and took a long slow inhale.

I went back to the clearing where I'd set up the tent. The sunlight blinking through the budding branches had softened already. The sun sat just above the mountains. When it sank behind them, it would get chilly. The woodpecker's rapid staccato rang like a small jackhammer. Ms. Fineday would say to pay attention to the woodpecker. It wasn't afraid. The woods were its home and everything it needed was there.

I looked for the best place to make the fire. It couldn't be under low-hanging branches, but I wanted some protection from the wind so the embers wouldn't scatter if a gust came up.

A rotting log about thirty feet long lay on the forest floor. I found another, shorter one and dragged it over to place at a right angle to the long one. I'd make the fire in the corner, between the protection of the two logs. I had no shovel, so I used a rock and my hands to dig a hole first. The sweet, mushroomy peat smell of the soil rose up. I tore some of the beards of dried lichen from the hemlock branches and set them among some twigs and small branches. Then I went and gathered some more, bigger branches. The woods were growing shadowy and cooler. The sun would disappear soon.

Making a fire was all about preparation. If you did it right, all you'd need would be to set a single match to it. Grandma taught me that. We built fires when I stayed with her out at her cabin on Gem Lake and Grandma challenged me to build a one-match fire. Even in the rain, I could do it, if I could find dry tinder, peelings of inside bark or grass.

Grandma died two years ago and the cabin was closed up now. We hadn't been there since she died. Whenever I asked to go, Mom said all it meant was work for her. Mice had overrun the place and the pump for water no longer worked. And Dad said it meant we'd have to rent a boat and trailer, since Grandpa had sold the one Grandma used and there was no road in. But I knew there was more to it than that.

We never went. I wondered whether the loons still made their nests in the cove by Grandma's cabin, or if the eagles had gotten them. I didn't care if there were mice; I thought the cabin was the most beautiful place I'd ever been. When I learned to drive, I'd go there myself every weekend, canoe over so I didn't need a trailer, and I'd live there like Grandma did, all by herself, all summer long. I didn't know if I believed in ghosts, but I liked to think that Grandma was living there still.

CHAPTER THREE

Mom said we should gather all our food so we'd know what we had. I had two pepperoni sticks and three pieces of Juicy Fruit gum. Mom had half a bag of barbecue chips and almost a full bag of Scotch mints. Dad had about a quarter bag of sunflower seeds. Then there was a block of cheese, half a loaf of bread, three apples and three granola bars. The apples and granola bars were supposed to be our afternoon snack before we got to the motel. We all had our bottles of water, too, but getting more water shouldn't be a problem, because there was still snow in places and we had the stove and fuel.

"It's a shame we don't have coffee," Mom said. "I don't know how I'm going to face the morning without coffee."

I poked at the fire with a stick. "We could make tea from fir needles. Actually, there's lots of things you can make tea from."

She smiled. "I don't think fir needles are going to quite cut it as a coffee substitute."

"Dandelion root. I think I've heard of that."

"I'll pass. I guess I can live without coffee for one morning of my life."

Dad came back and squatted by the fire, warming his hands.

"It gets chilly when that sun's gone, doesn't it?"

"What did you find up there?"

"It's rough, but it's a road. I followed it a ways. Pretty rocky. But the GPS is clearly showing the highway up ahead. I'm guessing it's about fifteen miles. I really can't miss it if I just keep walking south."

"Famous last words," Mom said.

"I'll get up at first light. We'll be out of here by noon, early afternoon at the latest."

"Well that's good because we don't have much to eat."

"We won't starve," Dad said.

"People can go without food longer than you think," I said. "We can't go very long without water. But as long as you're drinking water, you can last a long time. Gandhi went on a hunger strike for twenty-one days."

"I think that's an experiment I'd rather not try," Mom said.

"You've got no fat on you," Dad said. "You'd be lucky to make it a week." He circled my wrist with his fingers. "Look at that."

"Gandhi was pretty skinny, Dad."

"How do you know all this?" Mom said.

"I read about it."

"Anyway, we're being kind of ghoulish. No one's going to be starving to death."

"Speaking of that," Dad said. "What should we eat?"

"You're going to need something for your hike tomorrow," Mom said. "How about we have some bread and cheese now and split one or two of the apples?"

"Sounds good to me," Dad said.

❖

It was crowded in the tent that night and I was pushed up against the side, so my sleeping bag was getting wet from condensation. The ground was a bit cold, too, and I thought I should have put the tarp down first. And then there were the noises. There are a lot of noises when you sleep in a tent. The wind was up and every once in a while it gusted and a shower of little twigs and debris from the trees landed on the tent. I heard Dad start from his sleep, and then listened as his breathing went back to normal. Some time before dawn, it started to rain. Normally, I love the sound of rain on the tent, but I kept thinking of Dad, and how he'd have to be walking in it.

The rain woke Mom, too. I could feel her listening as she lay beside me. In fact, I think all three of us were awake, and we stayed like that, listening to the rain, until a pale gray light dawned.

"I want you to take the tent," Mom whispered to Dad.

"I don't need the tent. I want to be light on my feet."

"No, listen. You probably won't need it, but neither will we. We have the truck. I just don't want you out in that rain without shelter. Just in case."

"In case what?"

"In case it's farther than you think."

"It's not. The technology doesn't lie. I've told you before. You have to trust the technology."

"Just humor me then. No sleeping bag. Just the tent in case you need to stop and you need shelter."

"All right, I'll take the tent. That means I need my pack. I want to leave right away."

"Francie?"

"I'm awake."

"Can you pack up the tent for Dad, please?"

He had the tent, and he had matches, his GPS, one of the pep-peroni sticks, an apple and a granola bar, water. He had good hiking boots, waterproof. He had a hat—his Canada Post toque—then his hoodie, then his yellow rain jacket.

"You brought your work toque," Mom said.

"Gotta have the magic toque," Dad said. "It makes me walk faster."

This wool toque was a joke between Mom and Dad. There was a drawer full of brand-new ski hats at home that Mom had bought him for Christmas, and Dad had never worn any of them; he liked the old navy-blue and red Canada Post toque he wore to work every day.

Mom fussed over his pack and tried to keep the tears out of her eyes. Now that he was really going, there were no more jokes. It was only fifteen miles, and he walked close to that in a regular workday. But he was walking into the dense Oregon forest, and in spite of what he said about the GPS, he didn't know exactly where he was going or what might be in his path to get there. What if there was a mountain? What if there was a river?

I wanted to say something, but I didn't want to seem like I doubted him.

"Okay, Squirt," he said and kissed the top of my head. "Catch you later. I'll bring you a hot chocolate, how does that sound?"

He hefted his pack and pulled the straps tighter.

"Should we bet on how long it'll take me?"

"Never mind that," said Mom. "We don't want you rushing. It'll take how long it takes."

Dad grinned. "See, that's why I married you."

He winked at me and turned to the road. It was now or never. He took a step.

"Dad!"

He turned.

"I just wonder. You could always go the other way."

"I know, Squirt. But it'd take me two days at least. Don't worry. I'll be back before you know it."

So he walked away and disappeared into the curtain of rain. We watched as the trees swallowed him up.

CHAPTER FOUR

"You know what?" Mom said. "Fir needle tea does sound pretty good this morning."

"I'll go gather some."

"You know what you're doing?"

"Douglas fir is one of the easiest trees to identify."

"And you're sure it's safe to ingest?"

"We made it with Ms. Fineday. It's really tasty."

I could see my breath as I stepped into the woods. The ground was springy with moss and fallen needles and rain. It wasn't hard to find fir trees. The younger ones had branches low enough to the ground that I could reach them. I stripped sprigs of needles from the branches and the fresh, citrusy smell made me happy. As I held them to my nose, I remembered Ms. Fineday saying that you should thank the tree for sharing its needles with you.

"Sorry," I said. "I was kind of preoccupied." Then I said a proper thank you and stuffed the sprigs into my pockets. As I did, I noticed the rain had turned to snow—thick, wet flakes, falling fast.

Mom was on the tailgate, smoking, when I got back.

"It's snowing," she said.

"This needs to be chopped up to get the flavor to really come out."

"Might as well do it right," she said. "We've got time."

I got out my jackknife and laid the fir needles out on a piece of bark that was lying on the road. Then I chopped the needles as best I could.

I think both Mom and I were thinking about, or trying not to think about, time. Like how much had passed, or not passed. The first time I looked at the clock in the truck, it was only 7:30 a.m. I figured if Dad normally walked four miles an hour at a regular pace, which is what he said, then he might only walk three miles an hour through the bush, or even less if it was tough going. So if it was fifteen miles to the road, that's still over five hours of walking. If he'd left around six, and Mom knew exactly what time it was because I saw her check, then he might not get to the highway until eleven. Then he had to find a tow truck or whatever he was planning to do—he hadn't talked about that part. And it had taken us quite a while to come down that road: How many hours were we on it? He probably wouldn't be back here until after dark. I wondered if Mom knew that.

Sitting in the truck with the snow landing on the windshield and sliding down the glass in lines, we drank the tea I'd made on the one-burner stove. Mom said the tea was good, and

I thought it was, but a bit bland. If I made it again, I'd use more needles. I had used most of my water making it, but we still had Mom's bottle. The tea was hot at least; the air, even in the truck, was chilly.

We were each in our sleeping bags. I was crowded into the driver's seat behind the wheel, but the seat could recline if I wanted. After Mom finished her tea, she said she was going to sleep for a bit more. I got my sketchbook out of the backseat and worked on a pencil drawing of her. I wasn't good with eyes, so it was just as well hers were closed. I sketched her hair with long, smooth pencil strokes and I tried not to look at the clock.

When I finally let myself look, it was nearly ten. I was stiff from sitting so long, and I was getting hungry. I wondered where Dad was and if he'd eaten his pepperoni yet and if he was moving fast enough to stay warm.

The snow had changed back to rain again, a soft, steady patter on the truck roof. The windows had fogged up, and for a minute, it seemed as if we were on a boat, so far out to sea we couldn't see the horizon.

"Getting hungry?" Mom turned to me.

"Yeah."

"What should we have?"

"Split the pepperoni?"

"And split the apple?"

"We could save the apple for lunch."

"We've got a few barbecue chips."

So we sat in the truck and ate our breakfast of pepperoni and barbecue chips with a few sips of water and we tried not to look at the clock.

"I wish it wasn't raining," I said.

"Me too."

"Poor Dad will be getting pretty wet."

"I know."

I put on my raincoat and went out to pee. In the woods, the rain didn't seem so bad; the trees were catching some of it. I breathed in the fresh, rich smell.

Everything changes, Grandma used to say. She used to take me out to the woods, crouch down to show me the ants and beetles dragging grains of dirt and bits of stick and carrying them off somewhere. Sometimes I tried to follow them to see where they were going, but I always lost track of them. The wind blew leaves from the trees or they just died and dropped off and the sun coming through the branches made shadows that were always changing, and we changed, too, got too hot, or got chilled or hungry or tired, then we slept and ate and felt good again. She said it made her feel better knowing that nothing was permanent.

Sometimes I catch a glimpse of what she meant, like when I lay on a blanket in the backyard looking up at the stars. The stars are always changing, even minute by minute, and the stars you see at 9 p.m. are in a different place in the sky by 11 p.m. In the summer, Orion's Belt disappears, but in the winter it's back again. I knew they were changing; I could be sure of it. But sometimes, like now, seeing the mist rise up from the forest floor and shift shapes among the trees, it scared me to think that nothing is permanent.

"We can play hangman," Mom said, when I got back to the truck.

I knew she was trying to take our minds off the time.

I came up with *tundra*, and I'd hanged Mom and even put hair and glasses on her before she guessed it. Her word was *ridiculous*. I followed with *shipshape*, which Mom said seemed like two words, but if I'd had my dictionary I could have proven it was only one. When I came up with *cataclysm*, Mom guessed four letters and then said she had a headache.

"No coffee. That's what addictions do for you," she said.

I looked at the clock. It was just before noon. *I'll give him another hour*, I thought. When one o'clock came, I pictured Dad stumbling out of the bush and onto the shoulder of the road, checking his watch, knowing we'd be wondering, and he'd be sorry he'd said he'd be back by noon.

Then it was quarter after, and twenty-five to two and Mom was asleep again. I got out and ran down the road as fast as I could, which wasn't that fast because of all the rocks and because the rain had made them slippery, but I just needed to move.

When I got back, it was 2:30.

"I didn't really expect him back by noon, did you?" I said.

"No."

"All sorts of things could slow him down. He had to catch a ride on the highway. People might not want to pick up a soaking wet guy who just walked out of the bush."

She smiled at me. "He'll get here. We just have to be patient."

"I know."

"Should we eat our apple now?"

"I'm hungry."

"Me too. The first thing I'm going to do when we get back to civilization is have a big plate of fries and gravy," Mom said.

"I want bacon and eggs."

"Oh, don't even talk about it. I want a good coffee. Even a bad coffee would be good."

We started to laugh. We laughed like crazy people until tears were running down our cheeks and then Mom stopped and said, "I need a couple of aspirin."

"Dad left the first aid kit. I put it in my pack."

As I was getting it out I thought that I should have given some first aid things to Dad just in case. But by now he was in some gas station somewhere, or at a restaurant calling a tow truck and getting my hot chocolate. The hot chocolate would be cold chocolate by the time he got here. I wonder if he'd thought of that. I didn't care.

We cut up the apple and ate it with some bread and cheese. I was still hungry. We got out of the truck and walked up the road. The rain had turned it muddy and slick.

"Let's turn around," Mom said. "We don't need one of us to break an ankle."

Beyond the edges of the road, lichen-hung trees and rocky forest floor with ferns growing from the deadfall winked at us in the soft, steady rain.

CHAPTER FIVE

"Francie!"

I opened my eyes. It was dark. The warm fog of Mom's breath hung in the cold air.

"Is it night?"

"Do you hear that?"

"What time is it?"

"Listen. I hear a vehicle coming. Do you hear it?"

I listened. I could hear the gurgling of my empty stomach and Mom's sharp breathing. Outside, a gusty wind spit freezing rain against the truck.

"I don't think I hear it, Mom."

"Well, I can hear it plain as day. I've been listening to it for almost half an hour now. I don't know what's taking them so long. Unless they're taking a different road in."

I knew better than to argue with her. Earlier, I'd heard the truck door open and she'd gotten out. Then I smelled the skunky sour smell of her special tobacco. She stayed out there for a while and brought the scent of it back in with her. I had not opened my eyes then, just felt glad to have her back inside, close to me.

The funny thing about Mom's special tobacco was that it made her feel better, but it made me feel worse.

Mom sometimes said that when I got hungry and tired, I became "unreasonable." That's what I'd say about the way she became when she smoked. Like once when I was sleeping over at Carly's place, Mom phoned at two in the morning and Carly's mother came into the room to get me to take the phone call. Mom said then, in a whisper, as if she hadn't already woken everybody up, "Francie, did you take your necklace off?"

I was sleepy and confused. "My necklace?"

"Yes, Grandma's necklace, did you take it off?"

"Yes."

"You took it off?"

"I did. I took it off."

"Okay, good. Good. I just wanted to make sure you wouldn't choke on it in your sleep. Go back to bed now. Good night."

In the morning when Carly's mom asked if everything was okay, I said yes, that my mom had just forgotten to tell me something really important, which wasn't really a lie, and Carly's mom said, "Okay."

Nobody's family is as perfect as it seems from the outside—that's something I figured out. I used to think Carly's family was perfect—one girl, one boy (her cute older brother, Nathan), and nice, normal parents. Her mom works in a bank and her dad works out of town on the oil rigs. They have a big house up in the pine woods with a view of the lake and the Okanagan Valley and they have a swimming pool and a hot tub where you can soak under the stars. You can see so many stars from up there where the lights of town don't reach. Probably like here, if it wasn't raining. Carly's dad used to barbecue hotdogs and hamburgers when I went over there, which Carly couldn't resist even though she's trying to be vegetarian.

I could smell that juicy grilling smell now, mixed with the chlorine-pool smell, fried onions, fresh sliced tomatoes and ketchup, mustard. In the summer, Carly's mom made potato salad with crunchy radishes from their garden.

Okay, I'm so hungry now I forgot for a minute what I was going to say, which is that a few months ago, Carly's mom and dad got a divorce, and if that wasn't bad enough, when her dad moved out, someone else moved in, a woman named Daphne who worked with Carly's mom at the bank but then lost her job.

Carly says she's nice enough, but it's weird anyway. She sleeps in the guest room and every morning sits at the kitchen table in her housecoat drinking her coffee, smelling like cigarettes, with a book of crossword puzzles she works on until noon, which bugs Carly and would bug me, too. Also, because she smokes, she goes out on the deck, and the smoke floats in Carly's bedroom window. She can't stand the smell, but her mom won't say anything about it.

Carly doesn't know who exactly this woman is, except a "friend from the bank," and her mom isn't exactly telling them anything else, so they don't know how long she'll be staying or if they're going to be able to keep living in their big house in the hills. And Nathan hates having her around, because he can't walk out of the bathroom in just a towel—or that's how he feels and I would feel that way, too.

My point is that you might think other people's families look more normal than your own, but it's probably not true. All the kids Mom counsels at school probably think our family is perfect.

"Francie!" Mom whispered. "Do you hear it now? Listen, listen."

I listened. I still couldn't hear anything but the tapping of the freezing rain on the truck roof. "Not really. Maybe something."

"I can't believe you can't hear that. I think we should walk back on the road, the way we came in. They must be stuck."

I hoped that this was true. I wanted it to be true. I also wanted to do something. It was only eight o'clock at night and it was weird to have just woken up when it was dark but still early. Everything was upside down.

"Get your rain gear on. I don't need you getting hypothermia on top of everything."

Mom pulled our backpacks into the front and I turned on the flashlight. We didn't want to use the truck's interior light and run the battery dead, in case we needed it later. I pulled on my rain pants and my jacket, which was still wet, and Mom put on hers.

Outside, it was pitch black and cold. I held the flashlight and shone a path through the sleet coming sideways into our faces. We had to pick our way carefully, because the stones were slick with ice. A crust of wet snow lay on the road.

"It's cold," Mom said. "Are you okay?"

"I'm fine." After a few minutes I said, "You?"

"Me what?"

"Are you okay?"

"I'm fine, too. I hope I'm right about this. I don't hear the engine noise now."

"It's hard to hear anything with our hoods on."

"That's true." She stopped then and pushed her hood back. I did, too. The tinkle of sleet falling on leaves and hair and eyelashes and road rushed in my ears, and nothing else. I looked over at the woods on the side of the road. Creatures in there were hunkering against the weather, like we had been, hushed and listening and waiting for it to pass.

We pulled our hoods back up and kept walking.

We walked for about half an hour; I was starting to feel the cold in my face and fingers.

"We still have to walk back," Mom said. "We'd better not go too far."

She pulled off her hood again and listened. I scanned the road ahead and the woods on either side of us, but there was no break in the gloom, nothing out there except trees and the hiss of the freezing falling rain.

"I'm sorry, Francie. It must have come from another direction. I could have sworn it came from this way, but sounds can play tricks on you out here."

"We could go a little farther."

"I don't think so. We'd better walk back."

We walked back, trying not to stumble on the slippery rocks.

"This truck never looked so good," Mom said, when we reached the red Mazda. "Are you hungry?"

"I can wait."

"Let's have some water. We need to remember to drink water, even if we don't feel like it. And next time we leave the truck, we should leave a note on the windshield. We don't want someone finding it empty while we're gone."

I wrote the note on my drawing paper in dark charcoal pencil: *Please wait for us. We will be back in a few minutes.*

"Maybe you should write 'stranded,'" said Mom. "In case it's someone other than Dad who happens by."

So I wrote at the top, *Stranded.*

That scared me a little. It made me feel as if Mom didn't think Dad would be back any time soon. But he had to be back. He had the GPS and by now he would have had lots of time to get to the road and a gas station or a telephone.

As if she'd read my mind, Mom said, "It could take time. It feels like it's been a long time to us, but it may have taken him longer than he thought to get to the road. Remember that hike we did in Okanagan Mountain Park? That took us all day and it was only supposed to be seven miles."

"And we don't really know what kind of terrain he was crossing."

"That's right. And if he got to the road after five or six o'clock, it might have been hard to get anyone to take him out on this road. So we may have another night here, I think. Let's hope I'm wrong."

Mom pulled her sleeping bag up over herself and leaned her head against the window. I propped up my flashlight so I could draw. But after a few minutes, when I heard Mom's breathing change and I knew she was asleep again, I started to think about the kinds of things we might be able to find to eat in the bush in the spring. It would be too early for berries, I thought, except maybe dried-up ones. There could be dried rosehips left on the wild roses, too. Any of the leaves and buds of a wild rose could be eaten. It was late April. At home, the arrowleaf balsamroot was about to bloom; in school, we learned that the Okanagan people used all parts of it: the young shoots, the flowers, the roots. I wasn't sure I'd recognize it without the yellow bloom that looks like a small sunflower, but I might. The leaves really do look kind of like an arrow. But they mostly grow on dry hillsides, and this area seemed wetter than that. There were lots of other plants I could probably find that I'd recognize.

I wrote out a list of them on the bottom of my sketch: stinging nettle, devil's club, cattails, lamb's quarters, clover, dandelions, mint, tiger lily, pineapple weed. My mind drifted.

Funny how a memory can fade in your mind for a long time and then something happens and it's all you can think about. I listened to Mom sleeping and I wrote my list of plants and then I couldn't stop thinking about Phoebe. Phoebe is— was—my twin sister. She was born first, by nineteen minutes, so technically she was my big sister. Phoebe was born with a hole in her heart, so there's no way I should be jealous of her and how can you be jealous of someone who is dead, anyway? Sometimes I worry that I'm forgetting her face. I do still remember the smell of her—it's hard to describe, but she smelled kind of sweet and milky, a bit like clover. That's my strongest memory of her now. She had silky hair, curls, not as red as mine—strawberry blonde, people called it, which is nicer than red—and very green eyes and freckles across her nose. Well, we were twins, so she had a lot of the same features I have, obviously, but somehow they looked nicer on her, and even though I remember these things and I could just look in a mirror to see her face, I can't *really* see her face anymore. I have to try hard to remember.

She's been dead for five and a half years. I hate saying that word, "dead," because it sounds like she's just a body or something, but what else do you say? Adults say "passed away," which seems kind of a ridiculous thing to say, like you can't quite admit the person really isn't coming back, but "dead" is wrong, too; it doesn't explain how alive she still is, to me, and especially to Mom.

It wasn't true that I hadn't thought about Phoebe for a long time. I suppose I thought about her every single day. Whenever I heard something funny, I'd hear her laugh in my head, like the trill of a bird. Sometimes I thought of the way she imitated other people's facial expressions or how she used to whisper jokes in my ear when we were supposed to be sleeping, and how Mom would come into our room and tell me to settle down and let my sister get some sleep.

So, yeah, I thought about her. But what I meant is that I hadn't thought for a long while about the day she began to die.

I must have slept because when I opened my eyes next, it was light. It had stopped raining but the sun wasn't above the trees yet. Mom wasn't in the truck. The window was misted over, so I couldn't see out. I listened, sniffed the air for her cigarette smoke, but I couldn't smell anything. I opened the truck door and leaned out.

"Mom?"

To get out of my sleeping bag, I had to squirm across

the gearshift and sprawl halfway onto the passenger seat, then shimmy out like a snake shedding its skin. It was cold, even in my fleece jacket. I jammed my feet into my hiking boots and scrambled out of the truck.

I thought I'd see Mom sitting on the tailgate, but she wasn't there.

"Mom!" I called.

In the heavy mist, the woods dripped with last night's rain. Some twigs snapped with the weight of something stepping on them and then Mom was there, emerging from the trees on the edge of the road like a ghost.

"Mom! I was calling you."

She looked up and saw me. "Francie. Good morning. I'm sorry, I didn't hear you."

"Where were you?"

"I just went into the woods there to pee."

"Why can't you pee on the road? You don't have to go into the trees. You could get lost. People get lost just stepping off a trail to pee, you know. I read that about a woman on the Appalachian Trail. They were eating lunch, she went to pee and didn't come back. Her friends never found her."

I said all this in a rush of breath. Mom came up to me and brushed my hair back from my face. "Shh. I'm fine. I'm here."

I realized my heart was hammering against my chest.

"Where do you read all these crazy misadventure stories, anyway?"

"I just read them. It was in a magazine." There was a tremble in my voice and I took a deep breath to cover it.

"Dad'll be here this morning, I'm sure of it. That engine I heard last night must have been someone else. Kids out joyriding, probably. Hungry?"

I nodded, not trusting my voice to speak.

"Well, let's see what we have left. I sure could use a cup of fir needle tea right now."

She smiled, then we laughed and I felt better again.

What we had left were two pieces of bread, a bit of cheese, the bag of Scotch mints, a few sunflower seeds, two granola bars and the three sticks of Juicy Fruit gum. And there was a little water left in Mom's bottle.

"Is there any snow in the woods?" I asked Mom.

"There are a few patches of it, yeah."

"I'm going to get some for water."

"Good idea."

I took my water bottle and the pot to gather the snow.

"Stay within sight of the road," Mom called as I crossed the ditch.

"I will."

The snow I found was not so much snow as patches of ice crystals frozen into chunks like small melting glaciers. I used a rock to chip away at them and put the pieces in my bottle. There would be bits of bark and tree moss floating around when they melted, but it wouldn't hurt us.

Once I had filled the pot and the bottle as full as I could get them, I looked around for anything else we could eat. The soft, green fronds of a huckleberry shimmered in the mist. It was growing from a tree stump, but of course there were no berries on it yet, and I didn't know if the new shoots of the leaves were safe to eat. I gazed out into the woods. On this side of the road, the land didn't rise into a ridge the way it did on the other side. All I could see were trees—fir, cedar, hemlock—dripping with rain in the morning mist.

I circled back to the ditch and there, growing at the edge of the tree line, were some wild roses. I didn't see any dried hips on them, but I could walk down the road later and look. I pinched a few leaves to add to our fir needle tea.

"A granola bar and a few sunflower seeds. How does that sound?" Mom said.

"Should we eat both granola bars?"

"Well, I expect Dad to be here before lunch, but we could save one if you want."

"Might as well," I said.

"He'll bring food. I wonder what he'll bring." She gazed out at the road, looking thoughtful.

"A bacon and egger. Potato patties," I said.

"Hot coffee. Anything deep-fried. Donuts, maybe. Those ones with the powdered sugar; those are so good."

"I hope it's something hot."

"Me too. What time do you think he'll get here? Do you want to bet on it?"

I set up the one-burner stove on the tailgate, thinking about it. I put the pot of snow I'd gathered to heat while I chopped fir needles with my jackknife.

"I say ten o'clock," Mom said.

"Exactly ten?"

"Ten thirty. No—10:15. Split the difference."

I thought about 9:45, but that seemed too early if he had to arrange for a tow truck first thing. Most places opened at eight. If he left at 8:30, took a couple of hours to get down the road . . .

"Ten thirty," I said.

"You sure? That's your final guess?"

"Yes. Ten thirty. Even if he's later, I still win."

"You have to be within five minutes to win the prize, don't you agree?"

"What's the prize?"

"Dinner at any restaurant you want."

"Okay, 10:45."

"Final, final?"

I nodded.

Mom and I drank our tea and ate our half granola bar sitting on the tailgate in the drizzling rain. It wasn't yet 7 a.m. My neck and legs were stiff from sleeping in the truck.

I savored each sunflower seed, sucking the salt off the shells first.

"That felt like something," Mom said. "I actually feel better."

She jumped down from the tailgate and brushed off her jeans. Then she pulled the elastic off her ponytail, bent over and shook out her hair. Mom's hair was chestnut brown, a hint of copper red left in it. She was a redhead when she was younger, she told me, when she wanted to reassure me that my hair wouldn't always be as red as it was now. She straightened and refastened the elastic.

"Let's go for a walk up the road. We've got that sign in the windshield, and I can't imagine they'd come in any other way than the road we came down. Anyway, we need to stretch, get the kinks out. That truck's not the most comfortable place to sleep."

"Try sleeping behind the steering wheel," I said.

"No thanks. I'll be happy if I never have to spend a night sleeping in a vehicle again, thank you very much."

I put the stove away and we headed up the road again. I brought a bag in case I saw anything we could eat. I knew we probably wouldn't have to eat anything like that, but I liked the idea of being prepared.

By my wristwatch, we walked for forty-three minutes, not hurrying. I found seven rosehips and put them in my collecting bag. And I found lamb's quarters that were supposed to taste a lot like spinach. I put those in my bag, too. We might have covered a mile or a mile and a half. In places, I saw the stain of oil on the rocks where the truck had leaked. I didn't point them out to Mom.

When I found a patch of dandelions, I got a rock to dig out the roots. My guidebook said you could eat the flowers, though there weren't any on these plants, and you could eat the leaves and the roots. They were supposed to be healthy in the spring. I had once picked all the dandelion greens I could find on our lawn and asked Mom if I could make a salad of them. I'd chopped up radishes and some tomatoes and I put the salad in a glass bowl on the table at supper. Dad had taken a bite and then said, "What's this? It's a bit bitter, isn't it?"

Mom had smiled at me and let me tell Dad.

"It's a dandelion salad," I said.

"Where'd you pick them?"

"She picked them right in our own backyard," Mom said.

Dad got a choked look on his face and spit out what he'd been chewing, then drank down a whole glass of water.

"Dandelion greens are supposed to be good for you in the spring, Leonard," Mom said gently, trying, I knew, to let Dad know he'd hurt my feelings.

"I'm sorry, Squirt. Old Otto sneaks into our yard at night and sprays our weeds with Roundup. I saw him from the kitchen window one night when I was getting a glass of water."

"Oh my God, Len, why didn't you ever tell me that?" Mom said. "I go out there in my bare feet all the time and then I come in and probably track that stuff all over the house."

That was the only time I'd almost eaten dandelion greens. Now, as I dug and picked, separating the roots from the greens, Mom sat on a rock and stared up the road. She waited and listened. Clouds hid the sun, but the rain had stopped for now. After maybe half an hour, she got up suddenly and said, "Maybe we shouldn't have left the truck. What if . . . I hate to think of them waiting there for us. Let's go back."

So we hurried and got back in half an hour, but everything was as we had left it.

"I'd like to stretch out in the truck bed. We can put the tarp and sleeping bags down," Mom said. "My back is so stiff. I just need to be flat for a while."

We worked together on setting that up and then we lay down together to wait. I drifted off to sleep with the sky brightening a little, taking the chill out of the air.

"I hear something," Mom said.

I opened my eyes. The light told me that it was probably past ten already. I checked my watch. It was 10:38 a.m. Unless Dad arrived soon, I wouldn't win the prize.

"Do you hear it?"

"I think it's a plane." I was still on my back and I looked into the sky and saw it tracking west to east through low cloud.

"I wonder," Mom said, almost to herself. "I wonder if they'd bring in a plane."

"I think it's a jet, Mom. Look, you can see it."

She looked up. "What if Leonard couldn't find the road again. It's not on the map. He would have had to loop back from that other highway. It's possible he couldn't find the road."

I didn't like the way she used Dad's first name. It was like she wasn't really talking to me. Besides, if Dad couldn't find the road, it would make it his fault again and I didn't like that.

"There aren't that many roads, Mom."

She turned and looked at me. "Have you ever noticed how you say 'Mom' at the end of your sentences when you're trying to tell me I'm being a dummy?"

I didn't answer. I couldn't quite tell if she was kidding or if she was really mad at me.

"Like, 'That was a jet, Mom.' I wasn't suggesting they'd bring a jet out to look for us."

"I know," I said.

"And then you just did it again." She fell silent. My mouth went dry. It was better not to say anything. It was better to wait and it would pass.

Mom sighed and crossed her arms under her head, looking up at the sky. After a few more minutes, she said, "I'm getting tired of this waiting."

But we waited all day. We ate a dandelion-green salad with rosehips and sunflower seeds for lunch, but I forgot to take the seeds out of the rosehips, so they made the insides of our mouths dry and itchy. Every once in a while Mom said, "I don't understand what's taking so long." Then she fell silent again.

We fell asleep without eating anything more.

CHAPTER SIX

"Listen, listen, listen!"

"I'm cold."

Mom put her finger up for me to be quiet. She had the window open and her head cocked, partway out.

"I don't know what's going on but I know there's someone out there."

The noise I heard was close and loud, a high-pitched *beep*, *beep*, *beep*, *beep*, continuous, maybe ten times, then nothing, just the rush of a breeze moving high through the trees.

"What is it?" I asked.

"It sounds like some kind of tracking device. Or the signal when a truck is backing up. I don't see any lights."

The sky had cleared and was crazy with stars, more than I had ever seen, so many that the black looked almost brushed with light. We held our breath, listening.

Then it came again, a steady, high tone that sounded so familiar to me. But I couldn't put my finger on it. I counted more than thirty beeps, almost no pauses between them, except in one place, almost a hiccup, and then silence.

"Hello!" Mom called out the window, scanning the woods. "Hello! We're here!" She got out.

"Francie, get your flashlight. We'll shine it into the woods so they can see us."

I found my flashlight where I'd left it on the dash and climbed out of my sleeping bag.

"Give it to me. Hurry up." Mom flicked it on and swept the trees, first in a low arc then a high one. "Hello, hello! We're over here!"

She flashed the light on and off. "What's the signal for SOS?"

"Three short, three long, three short."

Mom fumbled with the flashlight and dropped it. It rolled away and went out. I felt with my hands on the rocks and found it again, gave it a knock with my fist and it came back on.

I flashed three short flashes, then three long, then three short again into the bush.

"Do it again. Keep it up. I'll turn on the truck lights."

As Mom went around and got in the truck, the sound came again, but this time I heard something slightly different. The noise stopped after every few beeps and then there was the slightest change in tone, followed by a little bark. Then I knew that the sound was not something human at all, but a bird.

Before I could turn to tell Mom what I'd heard, a mighty blast of the truck's horn shattered the quiet. I nearly jumped out of my boots. I clapped my hands over my ears. Three short, three long, three short blasts reverberated off the mountains and seemed to rock the ground.

When the horn stopped echoing through the trees, Mom said, "Anybody out there will hear that."

"I think it was a bird," I said quietly. "The beeps we heard."
I was careful not to add "Mom."

"That was no bird."

"I'm pretty sure it was. I heard it again just as you got in the truck."

"I heard it, too."

"It made a barking noise."

"I've never heard a bird make a noise like that. It was an electronic noise. Like a timer of some kind." Mom came around to stand next to me.

I wanted it to be an electronic noise, but I knew it wasn't. Mom hadn't heard clearly what I'd heard.

We listened again and the woods now roared with the silence, like the sound of the truck horn had shocked everything into stillness. Even the breeze had dropped. She took my hand and squeezed it.

"I'll leave the truck lights on for a while so they can find us."

But I had the feeling that she knew what I knew, that the beeping was not the noise of someone coming to rescue us.

It was almost morning. The stars had begun to fade in a gray light that seemed to seep into the sky like a dirty cloth rinsed in clean water. Back in our sleeping bags with the truck windows open, we tried to stay awake and listen. Mom fell asleep first. I shut off the truck lights. There were no more beeps, and I had almost nodded off again when a distinct, sharp crack of a branch snapped me awake again. It was close, in the trees just beside the road. Another one, and the low alders shook with movement. A flash of fear thundered in my blood, my heart knocking crazily against my chest.

I was about to shake Mom awake when an animal stepped from the trees. It had a big rack of antlers and it stepped onto the road, alongside the truck, and stared at me. I stared back at it. It was bigger than a deer, with a tan body and black neck; I thought it was probably an elk, which I had seen once when we drove through Banff. It just stood there looking at me, wondering what I was, and I looked back. I wanted to ask it a question, like, "Where did you come from? And do you know where the nearest highway is?" He put his head down and walked on, heading in the direction Dad had gone. I watched him until he disappeared into the trees and the birds began to wake up.

CHAPTER SEVEN

The letters SOS come from Morse code. Some people say they stand for "Save Our Souls." I woke up on Day Four knowing this, although I hadn't remembered it the night before. The words were in my head first thing as I felt the sun on my cheek and I opened my eyes: Save Our Souls.

Mom was sitting on the tailgate, reading.

A ghost of tobacco smoke hung in the air, but I wouldn't say anything. The more Mom smoked, the less I could say anything to her about it, a fact I'd learned from experience.

"We assumed that we couldn't get the truck started," Mom said, as if picking up a conversation we'd already been having. "That could be right. But what if it's wrong? What if there's a way to get it going? Even if we could drive partway out, it might be enough."

She held up the owner's manual for the truck.

"Good morning, by the way. How did you sleep?"

"Okay," I said. "I'm stiff."

"I didn't sleep a wink. How's our water situation?"

"We're going to need some soon."

"I wish we'd thought to collect it when it was raining. But we didn't expect . . ." She stopped and handed me the truck owner's manual.

"You know far more about engines than I do. Where should we start?"

"There's a thing called a decision tree. Dad told me about it. You go through these steps, one by one. One thing leads to another. I forget what you start with. Maybe battery."

One afternoon when he was working on the truck, Dad had drawn me a quick diagram with a pencil on a scrap of cardboard he'd been kneeling on in the driveway. I tried to picture it now and I could see it, the little box he'd drawn with two posts sticking up and a question mark over it. Does the battery have charge? I thought there was a step before that, but I couldn't remember what it was.

"We know we've got a good battery because the lights come on and they're bright. And the horn works," I told Mom.

Most of the time, a no-start engine has to do with battery, Dad said. He'd drawn a circle around his battery picture and scribbled in a bunch of arrows pointing at it.

"People start getting all complicated right away and overlook the obvious. Nine times out of ten, it's just a loose connection on the post. If it makes a clink," he told me, "or no sound at all, there's a pretty good chance it's either a dead battery or a poor connection, and that's good, because if it's the battery, it's cheap and easy to fix."

Was I overlooking something obvious? Would the lights come on if there were a poor connection? I didn't think so. They'd be dim at least, or flickering. It couldn't be the battery.

Mom swung her legs back and forth over the edge of the tailgate. "So if it's not the battery, what comes next?"

"The next thing, I think, is the starter. But . . ." I was thinking that it was probably nothing like that, since we knew the oil had leaked out. That was the obvious thing. But I didn't want to disappoint Mom. I knew she wanted to try something.

"But? . . . But what?"

We had seen the dark pool of oil under the truck. As much as I wanted to think my way out of this, I knew that there was little chance of getting the truck going out here.

"But—" I began again.

"But, but! But me no buts, Francie!" She threw up her hands. "If there ever was a time to be clear it's now."

Do you ever have the feeling that whatever you're about to say is going to be the wrong thing? I don't know why, but I get this feeling pretty often, and when I do, it's like whatever is on the tip of my tongue just gets caught and won't roll off. I don't know exactly when this started, but I don't remember it when Phoebe was alive.

There's a boy at school named Jack. I call him Jack the Jerk, though not to his face. Sometimes I go to speak in class and can't, and then Jack the Jerk says, "Frozen Francie is at it again." I give him my most furious, dagger-dripping look, because I think it's what Phoebe would have done. Phoebe always had more answers than I do, but I can't always guess what they'd be anymore. Anyway, it doesn't stop him, but it does make me feel better.

You would think that since Mom is a school counselor and she's supposed to be so easy to talk to, I would have told her about Jack the Jerk by now. But I never have. The truth is, Mom also gets pretty frustrated with me sometimes when I freeze up.

Now I tried to keep my voice steady. "I was going to say I'm not sure I remember how to check it," I lied. It was true I didn't remember, but that wasn't what I had been about to say. I was going to say it wouldn't help.

"Well, think," she said, softer this time. "Have a look at the manual. Maybe it'll jog your memory." She stared ahead at the road and I could tell she was sorry she'd been short with me. She was silent a few more minutes as I leafed through the pages of the manual, not really seeing them.

"Why don't you make us some of that fir needle tea? It's starting to grow on me. And we should eat the bread and cheese. It's going to go bad otherwise."

I turned the page on the advice that said, *If a light fails to illuminate, have the vehicle serviced.* An owner's manual, I knew, was not going to give any step-by-step instructions for how to fix your own vehicle. I set it aside and went to get out the stove.

"People aren't supposed to be able to fix their own vehicles anymore," Dad had told me more than once. "Not even the basics. Not even changing the oil. It's a status thing. You're supposed to be too busy to get out in your driveway or your back lane and slide under a vehicle and get your clothes and hands all dirty. You're supposed to just pick up the phone and make an appointment, pay someone else to do all that. But people are missing out on the pleasure of it. If you can fix your own vehicle, you've got some control over your life. That's why I want you to know how, Francie."

Mom jumped up into the back of the truck.

"Francie?"

I looked up from where I was digging out the stove.

"You were smart to suggest we save the other granola bar yesterday. I'm sorry I was impatient. I'm hungry and I've barely slept. You know I'm proud of you, don't you?"

"I know."

"You've got a good head on your shoulders." She gave me a funny smile. "You always have."

Some families hug a lot and I guess they say things like Mom just said all the time. But our family isn't like that. We tend to keep our feelings to ourselves and hope for the best. We hope that the other person just knows, and I think it usually works out all right. But it felt good when Mom said that. In the first moment, at least. In the second moment, I wondered why she'd said it at all and it scared me a little, because it was like one of those things someone says on their deathbed in movies.

I once heard Mom tell a friend that she thought she hadn't hugged Phoebe enough. She said she didn't grow up with a lot of hugging in her family, so she supposed it wasn't a habit she was in, but now she regretted it. You might think that she would then make sure she hugged me a lot more, but that didn't happen. Not that I cared. I got it—it would have been weird to suddenly start hugging all the time like she was afraid that any minute I might die, too. It would have been a bit creepy. Just like now, when the thing that was meant to make me feel better actually made me feel worried. If that makes any sense. If there's one thing I've figured out, it's that stuff in families never does make a lot of sense and you might as well give up trying to be logical about it.

The stove was lit. We had enough water for two small cups of tea now and a small cup of water each later. The bread had some mold spots on it, but I would toast it over the burner and it would be okay.

"What's this?" Mom said, holding up a small yellow box with some gauges on it that she'd dug out of the toolbox.

"That's a battery charger with a tire compressor on it."

"Okay, so not useful?"

"It might be if we had a dead battery. And if it was charged."

"Or if we had a flat. But we don't."

I nodded.

We sat on the tailgate and drank our tea and ate our toasted, slightly burnt bread slowly and silently. It was a warmer day, only a few white fluffy clouds in that blue sky that was the color that had no name.

I thought about the pool of oil that had soaked into the soil and stained the rocks under the truck and I thought about the clunking noise the engine made as it tried and failed to turn over. If there had been any chance of getting it going again, Dad would have tried it. He was good with engines, good with anything to do with vehicles. Sometimes he helped our neighbor across the back lane, a teenager named Duncan, who had an old Ford F-150.

If Duncan had a problem with his truck, he'd knock on the back door, a signature knock he had like a code, and say, "Is Mr. F-F-F-Fox home?" He was tall and skinny with eyes the color of Okanagan Lake in the fall, a little startled, like the eyes of deer I'd catch in the flashlight beam in the backyard some nights, and he had a mass of dark curls that gave him a slightly wild look. He had a stutter, so when he asked for Dad it sometimes took a while for the words to come out. I knew what that felt like, and sometimes I wanted to tell him he didn't need to bother; I knew who he wanted.

Dad said Duncan panicked whenever something went wrong with his truck, because he had a weekend job at a deli in Okanagan Falls, a twenty-minute drive south of us, and he was afraid a big repair would mean he'd have to take his truck off the road and he'd lose his job. I heard Dad tell him, "Don't worry. There's not much on this old truck you can't fix yourself. Nice and easy to work on."

I watched Dad help Duncan do the brakes on the Ford, replace the leaking radiator, install a new alternator, and I decided I liked Duncan, because he liked Dad and he always called him Mr. Fox, even though Dad said he could call him Leonard or even Len.

Although I hadn't thought it would help me to look at the owner's manual, I was getting to the end of it when I came across the diagrams of fuses and switches and then I remembered something.

"Let's pop the hood," I said to Mom.

"What are we doing?"

"I know how to test the starter."

I have to admit I had a moment of crazy hope. I could picture the engine roaring to life and us bumping back down the road the way we'd come with me at the wheel.

If we actually got the truck running, I knew that Mom would be driving, not me, but since it was my fantasy, I put myself in the driver's seat, and while I was at it, I had Dad walking up the road toward us carrying two mugs of hot chocolate when he suddenly sees us coming. I don't know why he would be walking, but I suppose it would make me even more of a hero to have to pick him up, too, and we'd all drive out to civilization and maybe I'd be on the news.

Once the hood was open, I checked the battery cables just to be sure they were tight and that there was no corrosion on the posts. Then, following the diagram in the manual, I pulled out the fuse for the starter relay. It was a 5A, so I pulled out the one for the power mirrors, which was also 5A, and I popped it into the relay spot. I crossed my fingers.

"Okay, Mom. You can try to start it."

The key in the ignition chimed as she turned it and my heart did a little flip, but then there was the same flat dead clunk. Mom dropped her head and arms to the steering wheel. I was so disappointed, tears sprang to my eyes and I tried to fight them back. It was stupid of me, since I knew in the first place it wasn't going to work. But somehow I'd hoped for a miracle.

For the next couple of hours, we ran through the other things I could remember from Dad's decision tree, although I don't think I did them in a logical order. I tapped on the starter with a screwdriver, swapped out some more fuses, and took off each spark plug cap and checked it, even though I didn't really know what I should be looking for, and each time we tried to start it, there was that wild hope that faded a little with each failure.

Eventually, Mom sighed and looked under the truck herself. "That's a pretty big puddle of oil," she said.

I nodded.

"Goddamn it! Goddamn it!" She slammed her fists on the hood of the truck. I could tell she wanted to say more, but she stopped herself. She took a deep breath and looked at me. "We better go find some water before it gets too late in the day."

We had two problems. How to find a source of water, and how not to get lost while we looked for it in the bush.

"Let's go." Mom marched across the ditch toward the woods.

"Mom, wait!" I called, then worried that I had said "Mom" in that way she hated. "I'm going to bring my compass and some kind of flag."

"We won't go far. We'll keep the road in sight."

"I know. I just think—I just want to keep track. Just in case."

"Hurry up, then."

I had a fluorescent orange T-shirt that would work as a flag. I dug it out of my backpack, along with the compass, a piece of paper and a pencil. I also strapped on my watch. I knew that it was easy to get lost even when you thought you were walking in a straight line. But also, if you have a compass, it's pretty easy to keep track of where you're going, so you can retrace your steps if you get disoriented.

Mom and I got lost two years ago, walking the trails on Cypress Mountain in North Vancouver, which seems crazy since you're practically in the city in that park. Maybe that's why we didn't pay that much attention to where we were going. Technically, we weren't exactly lost, since we were still on the trail. But when it started to cool off and we were getting hungry, we suddenly kind of woke up and realized we didn't know which way to go to get back to the car. Mom was mad at herself most of all. She said, "I'm the adult and I should have been paying better attention. But I just kind of zoned out for a while there." We ended up walking for another hour and a half before we blundered onto the road by accident. We didn't know if we were parked uphill or downhill from where we came out, but we picked downhill and we were right. We found the car after about half a mile of walking.

Mom had said, "That was lucky." And she was right. We had really only guessed about which way to go on the trails. We could have guessed wrong and ended up wandering out there all night.

Zoning out is easy to do when you're hiking. Ms. Fineday taught us that it's important to be aware of your surroundings. Are there any features like a big rock, a hill or a strange stump or tree? Horizontal things are especially easy to notice in a forest, where most things are vertical: a fallen tree that's caught in the crook of another tree, for instance. You make note of that so that you can look for it on your way back.

Even better, you draw it on a little map so you don't forget. And you can put a mark on the tree or rock for "home"
side and "away" side. Another thing she taught us is to look
behind ourselves as we walk. The forest looks completely different when you turn around and look at it from the other
direction, the way you'll look at it when you're heading back.
But most people forget that basic thing. Then, when they turn
around to head home, nothing looks familiar. And that's when
the doubt and the panic start to set in.

Mom and I looked out into the woods on both sides of the
road to see if anything seemed like it promised water—a creek
or a place where snow could still be. I knew a creek would
probably have more greenery around it, more deciduous trees
like cottonwood or willow. But we scanned the woods and
didn't see anything like that.

"Let's go north. We can keep the road in view," Mom said.
"At least we'll be heading toward anybody coming in."

I had a strange bubbly feeling in my chest as we stepped off
the road into the trees. It was fear, but also something like
excitement. I knew that it was my responsibility not to let us
get lost, and I knew that even if she wasn't saying so, Mom
knew this too.

We needed water, or would soon, and it would be out here
somewhere. But how far would we have to go to find it? Some
crows squawked in the branches. A chipmunk chattered at us,
then rushed up a tree and sat on a branch, scolding us. We walked
in a little ways. The straight, thin trunks of trees surrounded us,
with their scaly gray bark, black branches and beards of dry
lichen. Already, at that distance, it was hard to make out the gap

59

in the forest that the road made. You hear about lost people's bones being found within a few steps of a road. If you don't know the road is there, it's invisible. It just looks like you're surrounded by miles and miles of trees.

I took a compass reading, pointing at a rise of land in the distance, then marked it and the return reading on my map, where I'd drawn in the road. I wrote down the time.

Mom turned. "Stay close to me," she said.

The rich piney smell of forest wrapped us as we walked. I remembered rocking in a hammock, sun on the lake, waves lapping the shore and the sound of Grandma rattling dishes as she set the picnic table for lunch.

Pay attention, I reminded myself. But one tree looked like the next and the next—straight and skinny, pale lichen hanging from the branches like torn rags, like the ones by Grandma's cabin. I found the rise of land again and checked the compass.

At the cabin at dusk, the deer would step quietly from nowhere and their tawny shapes moved down to the lake. We would watch them from the screened-in porch as they bent and drank. Their ears would flicker, and they would turn to stare at us. I shook my head to clear the memory.

"Let's cross the road and make our way back up the other side," Mom said.

I wrote down the time again, took another compass reading and we walked toward the road. We were closer than we'd thought.

We got back to the truck without finding any water. Mom took a little sip from what we had left and passed it to me. Now that we were almost out, I found myself thirstier than ever. I wanted a big glass of cold water from the tap, full to the brim. I wanted cold iced tea, with ice cubes in it.

"Francie, there's something we need to consider," Mom said as she put the cap back on what was left of the water. She took a deep breath. "It's possible that there may not be . . ." She paused. ". . . that we may need to find our own way out of here. I still think someone will find us. But it may take a while and—"

"You said 'someone,'" I said. My eyes filled with tears. "Why did you say 'someone'?"

Mom looked into my eyes and went to speak, but I turned away from her and took off running down the road, south, the way that Dad had gone. I sprinted over rocks and branches and downed logs, dove into the thick woods and kept going. I could hear Mom calling me back. I ran until I couldn't hear her voice anymore, then I stopped. Blood pounded in my ears. Sun slanted through the feathery branches and splashed the forest floor with spots. I sat down in its light with my back against a tree. My breathing slowed and the tears stopped coming. Where was the road? I wiped my face with the back of my hand. Dad had walked through here, following what was left of the road. But there was no more road. There was just a dense jumble of trees, deadfall, rocks and hillocks.

I knew what Mom was trying to say. That Dad might not be coming for us. That he might not have made it back to the highway. What if the GPS was wrong again? What if the highway was not where he expected it to be? He should have taken my compass. I should have thought of that. You think you're walking a straight line, but humans always go in circles. Why is that? Is it some kind of ancient adaptation so that we'll always circle back to home? I stared out at the woods and pictured him hiking over logs and around rocks. I pictured his yellow rain jacket and his wet boots. I pictured him finishing the last of his pepperoni stick and I saw him turn and look to the sky, wondering. It had been cloudy for two days after he set out. The sun would not have appeared to help to keep him on track.

It dawned on me slowly. If Dad had gotten lost, he'd eventually circle back and end up somewhere near here. I decided that I would make sure I was here to help him when he did.

CHAPTER EIGHT

"There's something not right here."

I'd been staring into the fire, hypnotized by the flames. They twisted and leapt, then shrunk back and scurried along an edge of log, then leapt again. We'd built the fire bigger than the last one and more out in the open. If Dad was out there, I hoped he'd see it. We didn't want it so big that it was dangerous and we couldn't sit close to it, but it needed to be seen. You'd think that even a small fire in the bush could be seen from far away, but that's not true, as Ms. Fineday had shown us. If you're in among the trees yourself, you could be within feet of a fire before you'd see it, and if the wind was blowing away from you, you wouldn't hear it or smell it either.

Mom's voice had drawn me out of my trance.

"Something's not right here," she said again.

"What do you mean?"

"I don't know, something." She turned her head slowly and looked over her shoulder into the dark night. "I can feel it. I feel like we're being watched."

A shiver pricked up on my skin. The night had gone from pale orangey-blue to purple to thick blackness in the minutes we'd been sitting by the fire. We couldn't even see the truck on the road twenty feet away. Part of that, I reminded myself, was because we'd been staring into the fire. Also, the moon hadn't risen yet.

"I don't want to scare you," Mom said softly.

"I'm not scared," I said. But I only said that to make us both feel better. If I let myself be scared, I wouldn't be able to stop, and fear would lead to panic and panic was the enemy in the bush. Besides, what I was really afraid of was not the same as what Mom was afraid of. I wasn't afraid of being watched, or beeping devices in the woods. I was afraid that Dad had not found his way, that he was alone and still out there. After she'd come for me where I'd been crying and sitting against the tree, she gave me two Scotch mints, took two herself, and we sat sucking on them and not speaking.

Now that we both knew that the road Dad had been on had disappeared, the things we couldn't say grew thicker. Why had he not turned around? Why hadn't he come back? Trust the technology; that's what he always said. He trusted the GPS. He thought the highway was only fifteen miles away, and fifteen miles was a lot closer than the more than fifty we'd traveled the other way.

We'd made our way back to the truck where I worked on my map and Mom sat on the tailgate, thinking.

"What was that little neighbor girl's name, the one with the dark curls, remember her? A pretty name. Eleanor? Penelope? Something old-fashioned."

"Lucinda."

"Lucinda, that's right. And remember that time—you won't remember, you were too young. Do you remember how she used to sit on our back step when we were eating dinner and one night Phoebe saved some of her supper for her and brought it out to her?"

"That was me."

"What?"

"That was me."

"No, it wasn't, Francie. That was Phoebe. I clearly remember her balancing her plate so carefully as she carried it. You wouldn't have been six yet, you wouldn't remember."

"It was spaghetti and meatballs."

"Well, I know you two shared so many memories, but sweetie, you're wrong about that one."

Mom swung her legs and looked out at the road. Then she tucked a strand of my hair behind my ear and said, "That was so like Phoebe."

"She asked for more," I said. "And you called her inside and you gave her some in a bowl."

"Well, it doesn't matter, really," Mom said. "I was only remembering because of the spaghetti. It was so good. Those meatballs Dad used to make. He hasn't made them in years now."

We both pretended not to be angry. But after a while Mom jumped down and went to the cab of the truck and sat with the door open, smoking again.

I knew that Mom smoked to calm down. She called it her medicine. Sometimes it worked, but sometimes it didn't and it only made her worry worse and then there could be what Dad called "episodes." This started some time after Phoebe died. She would get caught on some little worry. I was going to say "silly worry," but I'm not supposed to call them silly. She worried about things that were real, but so small I couldn't understand how she could spend so much time on them. Once it was the furnace making an odd noise, and then Mom thought a strange smell was coming from the heating vents and she would walk around the house sniffing for what she called "poisons." Or like the necklace she was afraid would choke me in the middle of the night. The worse she worried, the more she smoked. It could become a vicious circle.

I'd heard Dad and her argue about it and he'd said, "I'm going to take that stuff and flush it down the toilet, I swear to God," and Mom had said, "Don't you dare."

Now, as we sat by the fire, I thought that I could wait until she fell asleep and then throw her tobacco into the fire. She'd be mad, but in a few hours, she'd come back to normal. Or it might take a few days.

"I think we need to walk out," she said. "I think we need to walk out now."

"We can't walk out. Someone has to be here when Dad comes back." I could feel my tears rising again. "I'm not leaving," I said, and I knew I sounded like a baby.

"This is going to sound crazy," Mom said, standing up and taking a few steps away from the fire.

I held my breath. *Then don't say it*, I prayed. I squeezed my eyes shut. I didn't want to hear it.

"I can't see a thing."

"Wait till your eyes get used to the dark."

She walked a little farther from the fire and I could see her scanning the woods, for what, I didn't know.

"Mom."

"Listen."

"Mom, come back to the fire."

"No. I can't hear anything when I'm sitting by the fire."

"You don't need to hear anything. If Dad comes back this way we'll hear him coming. He'll call our names."

She stood there listening. The fire popped and spat a burning ember onto the dirt. I crushed it out with my foot. I could feel the fear bubbling up in my chest like a pot about to boil over. I took deep breaths to try to push it down.

I wanted to distract Mom from whatever crazy worry she'd been imagining. But before I could say anything her voice came out of the dark.

"It feels like we're part of some kind of experiment."

I waited for her to laugh, the way you do when you've let someone else hear the crazy thing you've been thinking about that you know is ridiculous. But she didn't laugh. So I did instead.

"Yeah," I said. "Maybe we're in an A&W commercial and someone's going to pop out of the woods any minute with two Teen Burgers."

"Shh!" Mom's sharp voice came from the dark. Then there was silence except for the crackle and hiss of the fire. Then, booming clear and close came the hoot of an owl—

Who cooks? Who cooks? Who cooks for you-all? Three times. It was the same kind of owl we heard at Grandma's cabin at Gem

67

Lake, and hearing it now was not scary, at least not to me, because it made me think of Grandma.

"Like that," Mom whispered, so softly it was almost to herself. "Was that a real owl?"

I could almost hear Grandma's voice, speaking softly in my ear. She would remind me that when Mom had her "episodes," we could all be pulled in to her strange way of seeing things. But what was happening to Mom was not what was real. Remember that. I had to remember that if we were going to . . . if we were going to survive. And I thought that a hard thing—being out here, waiting—had just gotten even harder.

CHAPTER NINE

The first time Mom was sick, I was eight years old. It was soon after Phoebe died. I don't remember much, except that Aunt Sissy came to stay with us. Aunt Sissy's real name is Cecilia; she's a lawyer and she hates being called Sissy, which makes sense to me—who wants to be called Sissy?—but Mom said, "I can't help it. You were Sissy all my life. You'd feel like a stranger if I started calling you Cecilia." Which also made sense.

I remember when Dad and I visited Mom in the hospital. All she'd done was lie there in bed, sometimes with her eyes open, sometimes closed. I couldn't see anything wrong with her. She didn't have a cast on her leg; nothing was bleeding or cut. She didn't have a bandage on her head like you saw in the movies. Dad made a couple of attempts to talk to her.

"I watered the garden this morning. Your yellow rose is still in bloom."

Then there'd been silence for a while and Dad squirmed in the chair, got up, and looked out the window. "They're building a new apartment across the road. Looks nice," he said.

I felt sorry for him. Later, he tried to draw me into it. "Tell Mom about the birdhouse you made at school."

"I made a birdhouse," I said. She didn't answer. Dad gave me a look and I knew he wanted me to say more, but I couldn't think of anything else.

❖

The second time Mom was sick, I was nine. Aunt Sissy came to stay again. The first night she sat on the stool in the kitchen in her navy-blue suit and matching pantyhose and high heels and she said, "I don't cook and I won't clean, but I can microwave like nobody's business and I can hire a maid service to do the floors and laundry."

"We don't need that," Dad had said. "Thank you, but we're a twentieth-century family."

"Great, you're only a century behind then," Aunt Sissy said.

"I know how to cook and the laundry has always been my job. If you want anything ironed, though, you're on your own," Dad said.

"I didn't come here to have you do my laundry."

"Why did you come then?" Dad said. I knew by his voice that he was mad, but I didn't know why.

"Moral support. Company for Francie."

I was glad she was there, even if I only saw her in the evenings when Dad was at the hospital. We microwaved popcorn and watched movies and she told me about some of her funny court cases, like the couple who'd split up and fought over who would get their cat and when the husband got the cat, it scratched him in the face and he sued his ex-wife for turning the cat against him.

"I like having Aunt Sissy here," I told him one night.

"I know you do," he said.

"But do you like having her here?"

"Sure I do. Sure." He looked at me sideways and I wasn't sure he'd say any more. But then he added, "You know sisters. They can be a bit bossy. Mom doesn't always appreciate it. Let's just leave it at that."

That time, I was old enough to understand that the sickness Mom had was not in her body but her mind. It wasn't just little worries anymore. She saw things all wrong. Sometimes she heard voices no one else heard. Back then, Mom was new to her job as a counselor at my school, and adults who saw me in the hallway would give me these kind of sad-puppy-face looks or they'd say, "How are you?" But they didn't ask how she was, like they would have if she'd broken her leg or had the flu. It was all kind of hush-hush, like the time Ricky Maloney peed his pants on the field trip bus and the teachers frowned at us because we were all supposed to pretend like we didn't notice. I don't think I actually noticed this with the adults when I was nine, but when I think of it now it explains why I felt like punching my PE teacher or breaking Principal Vannar's thick glasses in half.

I did get in trouble once during that time, when I broke every single piece of chalk in a brand new box of it during lunch hour. And it wasn't too smart since I was the only one in the classroom at the time so they knew it was me. But it felt satisfying to hear each one of them snap, so I kept it up until I'd snapped them all.

71

Dad got called into Ms. Vannar's office and Ms. Gretchen, our teacher, was there too, wearing the sad-puppy-face and occasionally smiling at me with a frown and a smile at the same time. I thought they were making a big deal about nothing. I didn't think Ms. Gretchen was the type to mind using shorter chalk. But the tired and disappointed look on Dad's face was too much for me, so I made sure never to do anything else that would get me into trouble.

CHAPTER TEN

It was late by the time Mom and I finally climbed into the truck and zipped ourselves into our sleeping bags. I had wanted to keep the fire burning all night, but I was too tired. The reflection of the flames flickered on the truck windows. I think I fell asleep quickly.

I know I woke at least once because I remember feeling that Mom wasn't sleeping. I didn't say anything and neither did she, so I don't know how I knew. Maybe her breathing.

I jerked awake at daylight with a gasp. Something had wakened me, a bad dream, or my sore neck, or a sound. Or was it too quiet? I turned to look for Mom. She wasn't there. A muffled fog hung in the air. I craned my stiff neck to look out at the tailgate. She wasn't there either. I was suddenly wide awake. I tried to tear myself out of my sleeping bag, but it was twisted around my legs and I couldn't get out of it fast enough. I pushed open the door and yelled, "Mom!"

I fought with the zipper of my sleeping bag. Tears were springing to my eyes and blurring my vision. I half fell out of the truck with the bag still around my legs, caught myself with the side-view mirror and pulled my feet from the tangle.

"Mom!" I called again. "Where are you?"

Something was wrong. I felt it.

I ran up the road, stumbling over rocks, calling into the woods. She had stepped off the road before to go into the woods to pee. Maybe she'd done it again. I strained to see the blue of her jacket in among the trees. Could she be in there? Gray morning light seemed to swirl in a mist among the trunks and hanging beards of lichen. Nothing else moved. I ran down the road in the other direction, shouting for her. Then I stopped to listen. The stuttering drill of a woodpecker against a tree startled me.

I ran back to the truck to check the fire. Had she been sitting beside it? My legs felt like they were struggling through deep water. Ghosts of fog shifted shape around me. But when I got to it, the fire was cold. When I poked it, the embers sent up a thin wisp of smoke. No wood had been added or piled nearby. There was no sign she'd been sitting out here after we'd left it for the night.

Maybe she'd gone to look for water. I clambered onto the truck bed, cupped my hands around my mouth and yelled as loud as I could, "Mom! Come back!"

I must have kept that up for half an hour, my mouth dry with fear and the bad feeling growing in my gut. I paused to listen, then yelled again. There was nothing. The woodpecker's drill, the gray fog draping the still forest.

Slowly, sun began to shred the fog and warm up the morning. I remembered the horn. I climbed back into the truck and leaned on the horn. It blared in the silence. Four or five times

I blasted and held it. I was about to give the SOS signal when I noticed a folded piece of paper stuck under the windshield wipers. My heart leapt. How could I have missed it? How could I have been so stupid? Wherever she had gone, I'd probably frightened her now by blowing the horn. She would have heard it and worried that something had happened to me.

I jumped out and pulled the note from the wipers. Mom's handwriting on a torn piece of my drawing paper.

Dear Francie,

I'll be back for you. Don't go anywhere.
I know you'll be brave.

Love, Mom

CHAPTER ELEVEN

I threw myself down in the back of the truck. Then I cried like a baby. Like a real baby, with my mouth open, making as much noise as possible. I cried that way until my throat hurt and my head ached, and then, little by little, I caught my breath and sat up.

The folded-up tarp poked from beneath the toolbox. I pulled it out and opened it so I wouldn't have to lie against the cold metal of the truck bed. Even as I did it, it struck me as stupid to be arranging things so I could have a more comfortable cry.

When I really was a baby, maybe three or four, anyway, one of the times Phoebe was in the hospital, I remember crying hard so that Mom would hear and come to me. I remember stopping to listen for her footsteps on the stairs, and then starting again, louder, when I didn't hear anything. Eventually, I gave up, because I knew she wasn't coming. My crying in the back of the truck was a bit like that. If Mom was anywhere nearby, I thought for sure she would hear me, she'd be sorry for leaving me, and she'd come back. But after a while, I realized it wasn't going to work. Crying wasn't helping anything. She said she'd be back. Maybe she wouldn't be long. Maybe she'd heard a vehicle and was walking to it. Maybe she was looking for water.

My mouth burned with thirst and my head throbbed. There was a wilderness rule about how long you could survive without shelter, water and food. I thought it was three: three hours without shelter, three days without water, three weeks without food. But that didn't seem like it could be right. Three hours didn't seem long enough for the shelter part. But maybe it would be true if the weather was bad and you weren't dressed for it. Like on a surfboard being carried out to sea. I heard a story like that. That guy actually survived for two days, even though it was off the coast of Scotland or somewhere cold like that.

I was glad I wasn't on a surfboard in the middle of the ocean. Things could be worse. Sun winked through the fir branches and sparkled on the dew-specked grass and bushes along the roadside.

I jumped off the truck and hurried to the cab to dig out my water bottle. I had suddenly realized that I could lick the dew off the grass and shrubs. I brought the water bottle along to catch any drips I might cause by shaking the leaves.

You'd be right if you thought that it's not that easy to lick the dew off blades of grass. I found a couple of good drops on some plantain leaves. Because I was hungry, I ate the leaves after licking them. They weren't too bad—they tasted a bit like spinach, not my favorite, but I wasn't in a position to be a picky eater. I continued along the road, looking for dew and rosehips. I was craving a cup of fir needle tea. I thought that would make

Mom laugh. Maybe she'd be back by lunchtime and I'd make some for her with the water she brought, if that's what she was looking for.

You also might think that licking a bit of dew wouldn't do much to quench your thirst, but I did feel better after a while. I sat on a rock in the sun and chewed on some dried rosehips I'd found and I tried to make a plan.

The main thing was water. We'd been out here five days. Whatever the wilderness rule number was, I knew that water was the thing you could only go without for days, not weeks. In fact, the more I thought about it, the more I was sure that Mom must have gone looking for water. She should have taken me. It didn't make sense that she hadn't. Unless she had decided to walk out, which was possible. She may have thought she'd be faster on her own. Should I try to follow her? I stood on the road and looked north. I almost took a step. But the note said not to go anywhere.

It wasn't like we were in the desert. There had to be water nearby. But the dew had given me another idea. I could set up a still, using a sheet of plastic and a stone. Ms. Fineday had shown us this in one of our outdoor classes. She said even if you could find an old bread bag, or better yet, if you carried a piece of plastic in your backpack, you'd be able to get water in a pinch.

The bread we'd had came from a bakery and was in paper, not plastic. But Dad had put his backpack in a garbage bag to keep it dry in the back of the truck and I found it tucked behind the seats. I set to work cutting it open with my jackknife. Then I dug out the crowbar that Dad put back under the front seat and I used that to dig a hole. I dug in the softer dirt just off the road, but where it wouldn't be shaded by the trees.

It took me a couple of hours to dig it deep and wide enough. Every few minutes, I stopped to listen, hopeful. Then I went back to it. In the middle, I made the hole a little deeper. I needed something wide to collect the water in. The cooler lid would do the trick, but it was attached to the cooler with plastic hinges. I thought of breaking it off; I knew Mom and Dad wouldn't mind, considering the situation. But when I looked closer, I saw that it was held on with just one screw on each side. So I got the screwdriver out of the toolbox and unscrewed it.

I set the lid in the lowest part of the hole I'd dug. Then I stretched the plastic garbage bag over the hole and anchored it with stones along the edges. A small stone set right in the middle where the cooler lid was would direct the condensation from inside the plastic to drip down into the lid. It made me thirsty just thinking about it.

The sun had climbed to just about overhead. It must be lunchtime. Years of habit made me even hungrier at meal times, even here in the woods. If I had more to eat, preparing it and eating it would take up some time, fill the day. Eating, I realized, was a pretty time-consuming activity. Without it, I had a lot of extra hours to fill. I took out the last granola bar and unwrapped it. I was about to take a big bite, but something stopped me. I took out my knife instead and cut off a third of it. Then I wrapped the rest carefully and put it back in the truck.

While I'd been working, I'd heard the woodpecker tapping at a tree. Now he'd stopped and I listened to the wind shushing through the upper branches. No other sounds but that lonely wind sweeping the forest. As I ate the bar slowly, the creeping fingers of fear tightened a little around my heart. Saving that granola bar, saving most of it, that wasn't what someone sure of rescue would do. I didn't want to think about that.

I stood up and shook myself. I had to keep busy.

Down the road where Dad and the elk had gone was the way I needed to go to find water; I could feel it in my gut. But I couldn't make myself do it. Instead, I got my compass and water bottle and made circles out from the truck, looking, but not finding any source of water.

CHAPTER TWELVE

Mom had a funny story she told about how Phoebe got her name. After we were born, Mom was in the hospital for a couple of days. When a nurse brought her the forms to fill out with our names, Mom said she hadn't slept in nearly two days and she was a bit delirious. When Mom told this story, she used to wink when she said she was delirious and then she'd say, "with happiness, of course!" She had the idea to give us both names that started with *F*, since our last name is Fox. And her favorite sound in the spring, which is when we were born, is the chickadee whistling *fee-bee*, a high note, then a low note. So she decided the first name she picked would be Phoebe. But because she was a bit delirious, when she went to fill out the form, she couldn't remember how it was spelled. She thought it started with an *F*. She asked a nurse, who said she wasn't familiar with that name, but she'd ask around, and eventually she came back with the answer, written on a paper napkin by a patient down the hall. By then it was too late to change it to an *F* name, because she'd already decided that Phoebe was Phoebe.

"And that's how Phoebe got her name," Mom used to end the story.

Once, I must have been very young, I asked her, "How did I get my name?" I remember that Phoebe and I were both in the hammock under the maple tree in the backyard. I remember the sunlight winking through the maple leaves. Mom sat in a lawn chair facing us with her bare feet on the hammock, rocking us slowly.

"The nurse had come back for the form and I didn't have another *F* name yet. She said, 'Frances is a nice name,' and so Frances it was. Just think, you could have ended up a Philomena."

That was all there was to it? I wanted to ask. I knew it was babyish of me, but I'd always liked Phoebe's story better than mine. Who was the nurse? Was Frances somebody she cared about? Wasn't there any more to it than that?

I thought of this story as I teepeed sticks around a clump of dry lichen, then set a few larger ones around the teepee. It was not yet dark, but the woods had that bluish gloom they got after the sun went down. The wind had dropped and a deep calm lay over everything. I felt the chill of night coming on.

I had already collected a big pile of wood to last through the night. I decided I wouldn't sleep in the cold, cramped truck. I'd stay up all night and tend the fire so that Dad or Mom might see it. She'd taken her water bottle and her blue raincoat, maybe some matches, and nothing else. I couldn't understand why she hadn't woken me up. I know I said I wouldn't leave in case Dad came back. But I didn't mean for her to go without me. It didn't make sense. But then, she had not been making sense. And that worried me even more.

I knew, I'd known from the moment I saw her note, that trying to follow her would be a bad idea. If she had not done what I thought she'd done—that is, headed north, up the road—then we'd end up with three people who didn't know where the other two were. At least if I stayed with the truck, as Mom told me to do, she could come back to me if she either found some help or water, or if she didn't and decided to give up and return.

The fire caught, igniting the wood I fed it. I cracked the longer pieces in half with my foot and piled them on. Soon it was a good, crackling fire, the damp wood hissing gently. The night closed around me. Beyond the circle of the fire, the forest was a dark mass. Animals would be passing through the trees. They might stop, curious, and watch me for a while beside the fire. I had nothing to fear from them, I told myself. I was in their territory, not the other way around. I was just another animal to them, an odd one, probably, making this strange light flicker through the trees. I might hear the snap of branches, and that might be a deer passing by, or even a squirrel or a bird. Any sound in the dead quiet of night could seem very loud.

After a while, I felt my eyelids struggling to stay open. My head nodded forward and I caught it with an upward jerk.

The truth was, I was avoiding the truck not just because it was cold and cramped. The truth was, I was afraid to go to sleep, especially in the truck without Mom there. I was afraid if I got back in the truck, as we had the other nights, together,

I would not be able to stop myself from crying. And I didn't want to cry any more.

I tried not to think about her alone in the woods. Would she build a fire or would she try to keep walking? How far could she have traveled today? Mom was a good walker, too. She used to run a few times a week, although she hadn't done it for a couple of years. At her best, she could run six miles in about an hour. Maybe she would have run some of it. That would keep her warm, too. The road wasn't great and I wasn't sure what she had on her feet. Had she brought a flashlight?

I decided to check her pack. As soon as I stepped away from the fire, I felt the chill of the night. From the trees came the voice of the owl—*Who cooks? Who cooks? Who cooks for you-all?*

"Hello, owl," I called back. And the call came again.

"It's just me. I'm going to the truck."

Everything felt weird and slowed-down in the quiet dark.

When I opened the truck door, I noticed myself doing it, as if I were someone else watching me. I noticed, too, that the dome light was a little dimmer. I took my own flashlight from the dashboard and flicked it on. At the sight of Mom's pack, my heart dipped, like the dimming dome light. I fought the tears rising. Normally, she kept her flashlight in the outer pocket, but it wasn't there. I dug her clothes out of the inner compartment, as the scent of her, warm and powdery, rose up from them. Tears ran down my cheeks, but I took deep breaths and fought them back. I pulled everything out, her long underwear, her old wool sweater that she'd had since she was a teenager, her rain pants, socks and underwear. There was no flashlight.

I pulled on the wool sweater. Then I grabbed my sleeping

bag and pulled it out of the truck. The slamming door echoed in the night and I wondered if there was anyone down that long dark road who would hear it.

The sleeping bag helped keep the chill off my back as I sat by the heat of the fire. I felt reassured that Mom's flashlight was gone. It made me think that she'd been thinking clearly. She'd planned ahead. Maybe she would reach the highway by tomorrow. Maybe a logger or a hunter or a conservation officer would drive up the road and find her. Maybe Dad had broken his ankle and decided to wait it out in the tent. Thank goodness Mom had insisted he take the tent.

A new sound came from the bush, quite far away. A bird, a coyote or a wolf; I wasn't sure what it was. Something between a squawk and a bark. I listened for it to come again.

One side of me was cold. I tried to push up closer against Phoebe but her knees were digging into my back. The sun heated my face and neck. Phoebe laughed. She ran across the grass, daring me to chase her, but my legs were too heavy. I was stuck in place, watching her as she lifted and glided over the field.

A sudden pop woke me up. I'd slipped down off the log I'd been sitting on and was lying on the cold ground with my face to the fire. I looked for the ember that had popped from the fire and there it was on the edge of my sleeping bag. A jerk of my leg knocked it off and onto the ground, but it had burned a small hole in the fabric.

I would have to go back in the truck. If I wanted to sleep out here, I needed to build a proper shelter and I was too tired to do it tonight. I hoped I was too tired to think about Mom, too. I unwrapped myself from the sleeping bag, piled some more wood on the fire and went around to the passenger side of the truck. Once inside, I found the lever to lower the seat and leaned back. It was colder than by the fire, but I would warm up eventually. I pressed my nose to Mom's old wool sweater and breathed in.

In the fall, when the leaves turned yellow and Grandma and I took the canoe out on Gem Lake, you could almost think you were caught between two worlds—the real one above the water and the reflected one reaching down into it. I kept my mind focused on that, how beautiful it was.

CHAPTER THIRTEEN

A pattering of small footsteps on the roof woke me. Something
was up there, tapping on the metal. It was still dark. The fire
glowed softly, dying down, the orange light smeared on the
windshield. A few splashes rippled on the orange and I realized
the footsteps I'd heard were actually raindrops. It was raining!
I had not set up anything to catch the rain. I sprang into action.
The cooler could catch some rainwater. But if I wanted more,
I needed a better plan.

I pushed out of my sleeping bag, grabbed my flashlight and
jumped out of the truck. My breath made a fog in the cold air.
I had left the tarp half-bungeed onto the truck bed, along with
the few things that were still out there—the lidless cooler, and
some rope in a five-gallon bucket with a lid.

I jumped up onto the truck bed and pulled out the cooler
and the bucket. Prying the lid off the bucket, I fished out the
rope and tossed it onto the driver's seat. Then I stretched
the tarp out as the rain came harder now, stinging my face and
bare hands. It was thick, slushy, almost snow. I set the cooler
and the bucket on the ground and tried to find something to

attach the bungee cords to. I needed the tarp to be at an angle so water would pour off it and into my containers.

I brought the bungees up to the roof of the truck but there was nothing to hook them into. I turned the truck key and cracked the windows each an inch. Then I stuck the bungee cords in the windows and closed them to hold the cords and one end of the tarp in place. I brought the other end of the tarp down and attached it to the tailgate. The tarp was loose, but with a couple of rocks, I could direct the flow of water into the containers. I gathered two other fist-sized rocks, wiped them off with my shirt and dropped one in the bucket and one in the cooler, so that if a wind came up, they wouldn't blow over.

That done, I hurried to the fire and threw more wood on before the rain doused it completely. I gathered up an armload of sticks and moved them under the truck to stay dry. A couple more trips and it was all stowed under there except for a small bundle that I put in the cab. That would be my fire-starter. Then I grabbed my water bottle and held it under the stream of water running down the tarp. I shivered so hard my teeth chattered, but in a few minutes, my bottle was full.

Back in the truck, I thought of Dad alone in his tent some-where, listening to rain come down, no sleeping bag, nothing to help him stay warm. I hoped Mom had found help by now. I couldn't think about that. I turned my mind to the comfort-ing trickle of water running into the containers and I dreamt of canoe paddles cutting the water and rising, cutting the water and rising again.

CHAPTER FOURTEEN

Steam rose up from the cup of hot fir needle tea I'd boiled on the one-burner stove. I breathed in the Christmasy scent and took a long sip, felt it travel down and warm my insides. I'd taken down the rain catcher and then spread Mom's sleeping bag in the back of the truck, so I could sit with my back against the metal toolbox and the sun reflecting off the truck windows. It was a beautiful day, the sky that hard-to-name blue and sun streaming over the wet trees, making everything shine. The road steamed too, as the sun heated it.

My cooler and bucket were full to the brim with rainwater, and for a few minutes, as the sun beat down on me and I drank my tea, I felt happy, really happy. I had eaten the second piece of granola bar, the last of the sunflower seeds and two mints. Strangely, I didn't feel hungry. I knew I had to find more things to eat, but for now, I felt fine. I had a moment of guilt for feeling good when Mom and Dad were who-knows-where, but I forced that idea out of my head, took in the sparkling forest, breathed in deeply the fresh scent of the morning.

Ever since I was little, I had wanted to have adventures in the woods. On my walks to school, I looked up at the soft, sage-covered hills around Penticton and imagined myself climbing them, up past the tree line where the only trails were made by animals foraging for food. I read books about plants and stars and clouds and how to tie knots and use a compass and capture small game. Now, here I was, and all the lessons I'd learned had to be put into practice.

I gazed out at the sparkling forest again. I pictured a helicopter rising over the treetops, circling and kicking up debris as it hovered to land right in front of the truck. Mom, then Dad would jump out, ducking low to avoid the whirring blades, running for me with their arms open.

The road stretched away from me, a long, narrow ribbon being swallowed by sky. My heart began to thump wildly. Where was everybody? What was taking so long? The balloon-y feeling of panic shot up from my chest and into my head, making the road, the truck, the sky swim before my eyes. I was alone out here, surrounded by miles and miles of forest. I felt like I was the only one in the whole world.

Don't, I told myself. *Deep breaths. The sparkling trees, remember? Practicing my skills.* Then Grandma's voice came in my ear again: "Make a plan."

I had a plan. I took a sip of tea. My hands trembled. I had a plan. Today I would improve my camp. I made a vow that I would not spend another night in the truck. It was too uncomfortable, too cold and too lonely. At least outside I could sleep near the fire; I could stretch out with the three sleeping bags for warmth, listen to the sounds of other animals moving around me who were also trying to get through the night.

I swallowed the last of my tea and stood up. I needed to make a shelter. And then I stopped, looked out at the long road and I made another vow. I would stop daydreaming about rescue. A rescue could come today or it could come tomorrow. Meanwhile, I had to survive. That was up to me and no one else.

An ax would have come in handy, but I had no ax. I walked into the woods looking for something to make my shelter. I remembered my survival book, went back for it and leafed through the pages until I came to the drawings of shelters. I could build the teepee, the debris hut, the thatched hut or the lean-to. I chose the lean-to. It made the most sense for the materials I saw around me.

I figured I needed five branches for the frame I had in mind. Two of them needed smaller branches on them, like crutches, to act as braces. In spite of the rain, the forest under the canopy of branches seemed dry. When a breeze came up, the branches trembled and shimmers of moisture shook down through the sunlight. I breathed in a deep breath of the washed-clean air, spicy with forest smells. It *was* a beautiful day.

Working my way back toward the rise of land I had climbed on that first day, I saw that it made a natural boundary that let me know where I was, and although the trees sometimes obscured the truck from there, I knew just how to find my way back to the road. In fact, I realized that if I followed the edge of this boundary in both directions, I couldn't get lost. I'd mark my spot where I needed to turn in to get back to the truck. I gathered some rocks and built a little cairn, then planted a big crooked branch in it. Later, I could tie my fluorescent-orange T-shirt to it so I could see it from a distance.

South, the way Dad had gone, the brush was thicker, but there weren't as many tall trees. After a few minutes of walking, I found what I was pretty sure was a saskatoon berry bush. Though I checked each branch carefully, I found no dried berries on it. There were a few hardened like leather in the grass beneath the bush and I popped these into my mouth and sucked on them to soften them.

A dead branch lying along the slope looked about the right size for what I needed. As I reached for it, my eye caught something out of place in the bright green moss of a clearing a few feet ahead. When I got closer, I saw what it was: the picked-clean bones of a carcass scattered in the leaf debris.

It looked like a deer carcass that had been killed not too long ago, a day or two maybe. I recognized part of a rib cage and a leg bone. Something had cornered it here—a cougar? A coyote or a wolf? Maybe the strange squawking bark I'd heard the other night had come from here.

The breeze that shivered through the leaves suddenly seemed lonely. The bright, winking day, the peep of birds carrying sticks to their nests, it all went on as if nothing had happened here, as if Mom and Dad were not missing and I was not out here on a road far from everywhere, far from everyone who cared about me.

Oh, don't turn on the waterworks again. That came from the sensible side of me, the one who knew better, who knew that I could survive this if I kept my head. It made me laugh out loud, and my laughter sounded odd there in the quiet woods.

I had a lot of nicknames besides Frozen Francie. When you have a name like Francie, people find a lot of rhymes for it: Fancy Francie, Francie Dancey, Francie Pantsy and the double-special Francie Dancey Underpantsy. They didn't bother me. They were just word games, as Mom explained. But if I had to have a nickname, I'd prefer something better.

I decided to call this voice Fierce Francie. She would help to keep me calm. She would remind me that it wasn't enough to make the vow to stop wishing for rescue once; it would have to be made over and over again.

The bones of the deer would slowly disappear, buried by fallen leaves and new growth that would shoot up in the rain. It would take a long time for them to decompose. I picked up the leg bone and drew it under my nose, taking a whiff. It didn't stink, which meant it was still fresh. I'd eaten deer before, when Grandma made stew from the meat Grandpa's hunter friends gave them. But there was nothing left to eat on this. It was just a bone. A fresh one.

I once bet Mom that there was nothing healthy about Jell-O. (I was in bed sick and she was trying to make me eat it.) Turns out I was wrong. Mom had looked it up and triumphantly told me that Jell-O was actually made of animal bones, which turn into gelatin when boiled in water. That's supposed to be good for human bone growth. For losing the bet, I had to eat the Jell-O—lime flavor. Bright green. At the time, I wondered what could be worse than lime Jell-O. It tastes nothing like real limes. But what I wouldn't give now for a great big bowl of it. And it gave me an idea. Maybe I could use the bone for soup. If I could break it open, there would be marrow in it. It might not be too gross if it was boiled. I tucked the leg bone into my jacket and went back to gathering branches for my lean-to.

By early afternoon, the pile of sticks I'd found was starting to look like a decent shelter. I'd built it just long enough for me to lie down in, with a foot of extra room in case I wanted to store something. On top of the frame, I placed more branches lying side by side, as tight as I could make them. Now to strip some live fir limbs to lie on top of the frame and to add to the floor of my shelter to keep me dry and comfortable.

The work made me hungry and I decided to take a break to make my soup. I'd found some dried-up kinnikinnick berries, which didn't taste like much, but I knew they'd been used by Indigenous people so they must be healthy. Some fir needles and plantain would add some flavor and color.

My survival book confirmed that I could eat the bone marrow if I could get to it. It took a few tries, but when I wedged the bone between two rocks and smashed it with another rock, it shattered into three pieces. Again, I gave it the whiff test. It smelled fine. So I picked out the splinters and threw the big pieces into my pot.

I still had two full canisters and one part canister of fuel, but if I left my soup to simmer on the burner, I figured the fuel wouldn't last long. And I didn't know how long I'd need it to last. So I rekindled the fire and waited for it to get hot enough to have some good cooking coals. Doing these things, taking responsibility for myself, made me feel better——strong.

I was trying to decide whether to lay the tarp over my shelter when I heard the distant low rumble of an engine. I couldn't tell where it was coming from, or even what it was—a vehicle, a plane or a helicopter? It was distinct, but far away.

I ran for the fire and threw more wood on. Then I tore some of the fir boughs from the roof of my lean-to and threw those on too. A plume of blue smoke began to rise up. I needed more. I didn't want to smother the flames, but I needed big billows of smoke that someone could see from far away, hopefully get curious about and come to investigate.

But I overdid it. The boughs must have been wetter than I realized. The flames underneath faltered and went out. Running out to the road, I stood still and listened. It was still there, faint but steady like a tractor working a field on a sunny afternoon. It could be logging machinery; there could be a crew working nearby. If so, I had to get their attention.

I ran back to the truck and pulled open the door. I reached in and jammed my hand on the horn. It wasn't as loud as it should be—was the battery dying? I doubted it could be heard more than a few hundred feet away. What else could I use? I had a whistle somewhere. But they'd have to be very close to hear a whistle. Would the sound carry more than a horn? I couldn't think of anything else.

I tumbled into the backseat, bumping my shins on the gear-shift, and I dug through my pack, the contents spilling out everywhere. Where was the whistle? Why didn't I have it around my neck where it should be to be of any use? Stupid. Something metal clinked in among the crumpled clothes. I threw the stuff aside and noticed a slight gap where something had gotten lodged in the crack of the seat I was kneeling on. I slipped my fingers down into the space and felt cold metal. My fingers curled around the edge of something, and I pulled it out.

Mom's flashlight lay in my hand.

CHAPTER FIFTEEN

I would not let my brain go to the worst place.

It wanted to go there. Even as I thought of keeping it away, my imagination wanted to see what I was keeping from it. It wanted to creep to the edge of disaster and look over.

It didn't mean anything. It didn't mean what I thought it did. It could mean anything. She could have decided not to travel at night. She could have looked for the flashlight and not found it. She could have heard something that made her want to hurry.

Don't think about that.

My mind is a crazy thing. It can be my best friend or it can be my worst enemy. Fierce Francie said, "Don't hang out with your worst enemy. Who does that? Hang out with your best friend."

I needed another way to make noise. The truck radio? The driver's seat was piled with firewood. I climbed over the gear-shift and into the passenger seat, turned the key and tried the radio. Some static, dead air, more static. There was nothing; I was wasting time trying. It wasn't like the truck had some big, powerful speakers. They probably wouldn't make enough noise to carry very far or for anyone to think anything of it.

Drums could work. Our neighbor across the back lane, Duncan, his drums carried a long way down the lane when he played them in his garage. I could hear them when I walked home from the store. Sometimes I could even tell what song he was working on. "Smells Like Teen Spirit" had that ragged kind of hammering at the beginning.

Well, I could make my own drum. I tumbled out of the truck and pulled out the crowbar. First, I stopped to listen a minute for the engine rumble. Yes, it was still there. *I have to make this sound like something*, I thought. Something that would get someone's attention.

I made a few swings on the edge of the truck bed. In spite of the situation I was in, I didn't feel right about denting the truck. But I couldn't get any good sound from there—it was flat and toneless. I wanted something loud and ringing. I jumped back down and tried a hubcap. No good. Then I tried the tail-gate itself and that was better. It was hollow, so it rang out more.

I was useless at "Smells Like Teen Spirit." But I tried one of Dad's favorite songs, "More Than a Feeling" by Boston, and it sounded like something: Dun-dun-dun-DUN, DUN-DUN, Dun-dun-dun-DUN, DUN-DUN. I just hammered it out, over and over. I thought that if a crew was working, maybe there'd be somebody's dad who'd be having a break, maybe smoking a cig-arette, and who'd turn to his buddy and say, "Do you hear that?"

"That hammering?"

"Yeah, but it's not just hammering. Listen."

"I'm listening."

"What does it remind you of?"

"Sounds familiar."

"Yeah. It's 'More Than a Feeling.'"

I had to laugh at that. The chances of this actually happening? Next to none. But it was my fantasy, so in my fantasy the buddy says, "Huh. I think you're right."

And then, "Where do you think *that* is coming from?"

"There's nothing back in there for miles."

"Exactly."

My arm was getting tired and I thought it would be okay to stop for a while. Then I thought of one more thing. As hard as I could, I smashed out three quick bangs, then three with longer spaces between them, then three more quick ones. Save Our Souls. I did it five or six times to give the work crew time to figure that out. Then I waited a couple more minutes and did it again a few more times. My hand was getting sore from the crowbar.

I stood still and listened for the engine sound. Nothing. A breeze whistled softly through the trees, dropped to stillness, then rose again, sweeping along the ground and quivering the grass along the road.

I could hope, I did hope, that the workers had stopped to listen and talk it over. Maybe there was a girl working a Caterpillar, like Ms. Fineday did for a while when she was younger, and she'd hopped down off her machine and recognized the SOS signal. Maybe they'd decide to check it out. In a few minutes, I'd do it again, and I'd do it every few minutes and maybe they would find me.

I know I vowed that I'd stop wishing for rescue. But wishing for something, wasting my time daydreaming about something, was not the same as doing something to try to make it happen,

something that had a chance—a snowball's chance in hell, as
Aunt Sissy would say, but still a chance—of really happening.

❖

I think dusk was the loneliest time of night out there. I felt a
queasiness when the light started to fade, leaving a gray, empty
sky. A chill dropped down as soon as the sun disappeared,
which was around 7:30. Some crows or ravens seemed to start
up their squawking back and forth right about then. What were
they saying? And then they quieted, or flew off, and the other
birds, the woodpeckers and jays, quieted too. Even the squir-
rels stopped chattering. I sat by the fire and finished my soup.
It needed salt. It was probably good for me, though. I knew
I should go and gather some more of the bones while they
were still good, but when I looked into the woods, it was gray
and gloomy. The stillness rattled through me, empty as the
sky. I didn't want to go into the woods or anywhere away
from this fire.

Dusk was when I had to admit that no one was coming
for me today. Night would fall and I would be alone. Dusk was
also when my mind drifted into the shadow places I didn't
want to go. I saw Mom running toward Phoebe. I saw her bend
over her and brush the hair from her face. She sat her up and
folded her in her arms.

I wanted Mom to hug me, too. I was scared. I ran across
the grass to where Mom was holding Phoebe. Grandma called
to me. I looked back and Grandma waved me toward her with
her arm outstretched. But I was already there. Mom looked up

at me. She lay Phoebe down gently. Then she stood up, dug her fingers into my shoulders and shook me hard.

"What did I tell you?" she screamed. "I told you and I told you. No running. No chasing her. She's not strong like you."

Was it true? Was I strong? Why did she make it sound like a bad thing? Is there such a thing as being too strong? Sometimes I thought if I were weaker, like Phoebe was, Mom would love me better. Did she leave me out here alone because she thought I was strong enough? If that was true, maybe it was better to be weak. But that couldn't be right.

It was amazing what I could hear once night came on. At night, what I could see narrowed: the campfire and the stars. But I could hear everything around me, louder it seemed, than in the daytime. Even with the crackling fire, the frogs grew loud as dusk fell. There was another whistling noise, rhythmic, constant, maybe some insect or bird. Something was scratching around the truck. Once in a while I heard a little tick or a ping of metal. Whatever it was, it wasn't big.

I heard wind when it picked up and brushed softly through the treetops, and I heard it fall quiet, then rise again, like someone breathing or moaning. The fire snapped and sighed. But what I didn't hear was the rumble of an engine. No human voices or footfalls in the dirt. I had to face it—my drum hadn't worked. It hadn't attracted attention. It must not have been loud enough.

There was no point in trying to attract attention at night.

No one would be out here. No one would be looking for me. It was too early for anyone to be searching for us, and also, I had to admit that if they did start to search, they would probably be looking in the Grand Canyon and not here. I couldn't think of anything that would give anyone a clue that we were here.

We had set out from home early on the same day the truck broke down on this road. We'd stopped in Yakima, Washington, for snacks. I wasn't sure where we'd gone from there. Then sometime a couple of hours later maybe, we stopped for gas in that little town where we took the wrong road. What town was it? I hadn't even noticed.

Dad had paid cash for the gas because he said the bank dinged you every time you used a card in the States. So there was no chance we could be traced by our bank records, like you sometimes hear about on the news when people are missing. We hadn't talked to anyone. Why would anyone think we'd be here?

I stepped away from the fire and into the falling darkness. Stepping away from the fire even that far made me uneasy. It wasn't fear exactly, but that loneliness, gripped by the chill dusk. I took a quick look down the road in both directions. A broad pale path hemmed in east and west by tall black firs. Light fading fast from the sky. A bright star or planet near the horizon in the south. What did I expect to see?

The map was still on the dashboard where Mom had left it. I hurried back to the fire and spread the map on my knees, flicking on the flashlight.

The nearest town appeared to be Bend, but that was as the crow flies. I didn't think we had driven through Bend. It was east of where I was now, I was pretty sure. Between the town and here could be anything; it was hard to tell. Walking it was out of the question. If I were going to walk anywhere, it would be back down the road we came in on. But Mom's note said to stay here. To wait for her. I had to give her time.

Lying on my side, I watched the embers glow blue then red then orange then red. I pulled the sleeping bags tighter around my head, not because I was cold, but just to keep out the loneliness. The night hissed and ticked and whispered. Tomorrow maybe. Something might happen tomorrow. Dad with his mailbag on his shoulder coming up the front step, holding paper cups of hot chocolate, one in each hand. A bag of sugar donuts. Duncan's drums hammering out "More Than a Feeling" while I skipped down the back lane, the sage-covered hills around Penticton lit up in golden light. Soft piano music tinkling like water over rocks in a stream, Grandma on the piano bench, her shoulders rising and falling.

I sat up. I'd been nearly asleep. My heartbeat throbbed through my whole body, making my head ring. I stuck my fingers in my ears and shook them. I was really hearing it, piano music, faint but real, classical piano like Grandma played on her piano in the cabin at Gem Lake. But that was impossible. I grabbed my flashlight and shone the beam out to the road.

"Hello? Is someone there? Hello!"

I stood up and listened. The wind moaned softly, and below it, just as softly, the piano played on. I walked toward the truck.

As I did, the music got louder. Then I knew. I opened the truck door. Sure enough, the radio was lit up and the music was coming from it. I swallowed and tried to steady my quaking body. The heartbeat pounding behind my eyes slowly calmed.

I had forgotten to turn off the truck when I was trying to make noise. Strange that out here, in the middle of the forest, the radio would tune in on this sweet, tinkling piano music. But the sky was very clear, radiant with millions of stars. Maybe on a clear night, a radio could pick up signals from far away.

Grandma still sat there in my mind, her long silver braid twisting down the back of her turquoise sweater, her shoulders rising and falling. She'd play anything and everything, she said. "La Vie en Rose," Debussy's Arabesques, something called the "Root Beer Rag," and "River" by Joni Mitchell, which made me feel like crying. Those were some of my favorites. Sometimes I sat on the piano bench with her and she taught me to play a little accompaniment, just a few keys, easy stuff. Grandma had the most beautiful hands you ever saw—long, slender brown fingers, straight and fine. In the couple of years before she died, she used to rub them and pull on them; she was getting arthritis, she said, but she could still travel up and down the piano keys at lightning speed, swaying like a crazy woman on the fast songs and ending with a big rambunctious finish that made her and me both laugh.

The piano on the radio started to falter and fade out as I leaned against the truck, listening. It came back as clear as before, then just as suddenly as it had begun, it dropped out and was gone. Though I fiddled with the dial a long time, I couldn't get the signal back.

CHAPTER SIXTEEN

I didn't sleep too well that night. My lean-to was nice and cozy, but after the piano music, I kept waking up every hour or so, listening—what was that? A cracking branch? Or did I just dream that? The rustle in the leaves was real. But I knew that tiny birds made a lot of noise if you listened carefully. The third or fourth time I woke up, the moon was up, not quite three-quarters full. Silver light bathed the road. The truck windshield shone. My fire had burned down, but with three sleeping bags and a good bed of fir boughs as insulation, I wasn't cold. The trees cast slender moon shadows.

Then a long, low whimper rose out of the night and grew to a high-pitched howl. The sound quavered in the air like violin strings vibrating. That cry came from the south. A few seconds later, from the north, came answering howls, a whole frantic chorus of them. It lasted maybe three minutes, the whole forest ringing with coyote voices, yipping and yowling like they were trying to outdo each other. After that one crazy burst of singing, the coyotes fell quiet, though I lay there in my lean-to listening for them and wondering if they were moving this way.

I'm not afraid of coyotes. We hear them at home out in the hills, singing their songs. I like the sound. Mom and I go out on the step to listen. We try to guess if they sound happy or lonely. If there's a single voice crying, Mom says it sounds broken-hearted. I don't like to think about that. Anyway, even though I'm not afraid of them normally, it was different lying in a sleeping bag under the stars with just a bunch of sticks covering me.

I had my fire-poking stick beside me. I used it to poke the embers back to life and I threw on a few small branches. The flames twisted, surging and ebbing, popping with a shower of sparks. I drifted, dreamed of Phoebe running across the grass, rising into the air like a dragonfly skimming across the green-glass surface of the lake.

I woke to the shrill pitch of the beeping bird, its steady annoying tone like an alarm clock. Barely light. I sat up and wrapped my sleeping bag closer. Other birds were awake, making noises I'd never heard before: coos and twerps and chatters and clacks. The Oregon jungle. An edge of my sleeping bag was wet with dew, but the rest of me had stayed dry. Except for a dent in my hip where a branch had poked through, I felt pretty good. My braids had twigs in them. I hadn't brushed my teeth in days, and I hadn't eaten enough to keep a bird alive, but still. I felt okay.

It was Day Seven. Mom left at first light on Day Five. That meant she'd had two solid days of walking. If it was about sixty miles to the highway, well, it's possible she could have walked for ten hours each day, and possible she could have covered thirty miles on each of those days. Not likely, but possible. Let's say she was only able to cover twenty miles a day, which is more reasonable. That meant another whole day at least before she'd reach the road. Plus the time to find someone to drive back down and get me. And that was all the time I was going to allow myself to spend thinking about rescue. It would probably not come today, so I needed to turn my attention to something else.

First, I had decided, just as I drifted back to sleep last night for the third time, that I would unhook the truck battery. There was a little juice left in it and I might as well save it, for what, I didn't know. I popped the hood and got out a crescent wrench. The bolts loosened easily and I flipped the connections off the posts. Something seemed to be draining it, but besides the radio, I didn't know what it was. It might make no difference whatsoever. But I knew that when Dad put his motorcycle away for the winter, he took the battery out.

I'd been trying to keep my mind off pancakes. It kept drifting there and lingering. Aunt Sissy couldn't cook much, but she made the best pancakes I've ever had and she made them from scratch. Just for fun, and to torture myself, I tried to remember what was in them. Eggs, milk, flour. Baking soda? Or baking powder? I can never get those two straight.

Once, I tried to make carrot muffins and I used baking soda instead of baking powder. When they came out of the oven flat and hard, I stood in the middle of the kitchen and cried.

"What happened?" Mom asked.

"I . . ."

She crouched down to look in my face and waited as I struggled to get the words to roll off my tongue.

"I . . ."

Then she folded me in her soft powder-scented arms. I nestled in the warm crook of her neck and let myself blubber like a baby, and I knew, and she probably did too, that I wasn't crying over spoiled muffins anymore.

"Chh, chh, that's enough," she said. Then she drew her fingers across my cheeks to wipe away my tears.

"That's okay, Francie," she said. "If everything turns out perfect the first time, how will you learn?" Then, even though we used the last egg and almost all of the flour, and even though I had to grate more carrots, Mom helped me make the muffins all over again. That second time, they did turn out perfectly. I iced them with vanilla sour cream frosting, which Dad said was his new favorite.

I tried to decide now which I wanted more: carrot muffins or pancakes? I still think I'd go for the pancakes. Aunt Sissy puts blueberries in them and cooks them just until they're golden brown, a bit crispy on the edges. A pat of butter, and when that's melted, a glop of maple syrup that spreads on the hot pancakes and puddles on the edge of the plate.

I bent over my firepit and tented some twigs around a clump of dry lichen. I set a match to it and watched it smoke and then, with a little puff, billow into flame. I added more sticks as those caught, bigger branches. Instead of pancakes, I'd be having fir needle tea, the last piece of granola bar and a few mints.

Once the fire was burning nicely, I went to the truck for the tea things, granola bar and mints. The bag of mints was still nearly half full. The mints had been Mom's snack, what she'd bought for herself when we'd stopped early into our trip. She'd left them here for me. I don't think she'd even taken any along for herself. That proved she loved me, didn't it? If she didn't love me, she would have taken them with her; she wouldn't have cared about what I had left to eat. The Scotch mints and also the note. The only reason she'd gone alone and left the note telling me to wait was because she didn't want to put me in danger. And that proved she loved me, too.

My task for Day Seven was to find more to eat. That meant retrieving as many of the deer bones as I could for more soup. I had the bucket and the cooler nearly full of water, so soup made sense. Also, hot soup felt comforting, like real food.

After my breakfast, I put on my backpack, slung my compass around my neck and slipped my jackknife in my pocket. I also remembered to bring my fluorescent orange T-shirt so I could hang it from the marker where my trail led back to the truck. Would bones go bad? I had no idea. But I figured that since they hadn't hurt me so far, they'd last me another couple of days at least. Some kind of root would add some bulk to my diet, but I was less sure of roots than leaves and berries. I'd never eaten any roots from the wild, and I needed to be careful I didn't poison myself.

I was starting to recognize my trail through the woods. A fallen tree caught in the crook of two standing trees pointed in the direction of the little hill. A big rock with its top covered in moss lay about twenty feet beyond that. It didn't look like it had any handholds or footholds, but it would be the kind of thing I'd try to climb, normally.

A breeze whispered through the trees, wafting a soft warmth. The breeze came from the south. I could feel that the day would warm up, which made me think of Mom. I hoped she'd found water. She shouldn't have done what she was doing; she shouldn't be trying to walk out on her own. If she'd asked me, I'd have told her so. I could have convinced her we were better off to stay put. Maybe that was why she didn't wake me up. Maybe she knew I'd try to talk her out of it.

What day was it? I counted them off on my fingers. Friday. Yesterday was the first of May. By now we should have been halfway through our Grand Canyon hike. Friday we had planned to be starting back up out of the canyon. Dad and I had planned it together, leaving lots of time for rests, since we weren't used to hiking in heat. In early May, though, there could still be snow. It would have been a challenge, but we'd all have been together.

I'd been daydreaming again. Before I knew it, I was at the base of the hill and the rock cairn I'd made. I took out my orange T-shirt and tied it to the stick, then I headed south, watching for the clearing where I'd found the bones.

I didn't have far to go. I recognized the slope where I'd found the branch for my lean-to frame. Sunlight lit up the grassy patch below it. I pushed through some low shrubs into the clearing. But the bones weren't there. The rib cage was gone. The leg bones, the knotty spine pieces that I'd seen—all of them were gone.

I was confused. I was absolutely, positively sure this was the same spot. But it couldn't be. There'd been most of a skeleton here, a big one. How could it be gone? I must have the wrong spot. Things could be deceiving in the forest; I knew that. One grassy clearing can easily look like another. I should have marked it with something. I should have thought of that.

I bent and had a closer look at the grass, thinking I might see my own footsteps, or some evidence that I'd been there before. As I crouched, combing my fingers through the grass, the sun heating my hair, a shiver crept over me. The roots of my hair tingled. Something had been here. Someone. Someone had dragged away what was left of the bones.

I stood up and shook myself. *Don't let your imagination get carried away*, I told myself. This wasn't the spot; that's all there was to it. I thought it was, but I was wrong. I looked behind me. Leaves quivered in the breeze. My orange T-shirt stood like a beacon in the distance. A sudden *whop-whop-whop* above my head startled me, but it was just an eagle, his wings churning the air as he rose and circled. I took a few steps farther along the bottom of the slope. But to go any farther, I'd have to skirt the dense brush and scramble over deadfall. And I knew I hadn't done that yesterday.

I started back to the truck slowly at first, with the sense of eyes on my back. I picked up speed until I was almost running. Then I *was* running, all out, my lungs burning like they'd explode. I burst out of the trees and ran down and up the ditch and onto the road. I got to the truck, yanked open the door and swept all the wood I'd stockpiled onto the ground. Don't ask me why. People do stupid stuff when they're scared and I was scared.

I sat in the truck with my head on the steering wheel and I sat that way for a long time, tears like a tangle of wet wool clogging my throat. I didn't cry. *Sad* is too small a word for what I felt. I felt blown up. Like what you see in the news when a bomb's gone off and everything is in unrecognizable pieces and the "victims," as they call them, are wandering around like zombies in the wreckage. But you can't really go around that way for long. It just doesn't work.

Before long, thoughts began to push their way back in. Like that the truck was hot, the sun beating through the windshield. That the windows were electric and that that was a stupid design. What if your vehicle veered off the road and landed in the lake and you couldn't get out because the windows were electric? Dad said a crank window had been a good idea in the first place. Who was so lazy that they couldn't roll down their own window, and needed a motor to do it for them?

I sniffed and caught a gulp of air. I hadn't noticed I'd been holding my breath. Not everything new that humans invent is better than the thing before it. Pencil sharpeners. The little tiny ones you can hold in the palm of your hand and they're made of metal or plastic and can sharpen two or three different sizes of pencils. My grade-five teacher had a pencil sharpener on her desk that was the size of a brick and took batteries, I don't know how many. Like it's so hard to turn your pencil three times with your own hand to sharpen it.

Or coffee percolators. Well, I wouldn't know since I didn't drink coffee, but Mom said you couldn't make a better cup of coffee than with the old percolators you put on the stove. We had one we brought camping and it was all black from the fire, and Mom said it was one of her favorite things about camping—the coffee. But we didn't bring that percolator on this trip.

And Dad found a plastic Big Gulp cup on our front lawn one morning and he laughed about it and said he'd keep it for his painting projects since it was so huge. He said take-out cups used to be paper and they were about as high as your fist. And he said he didn't remember being thirsty after drinking one of those Dixie cups of soda.

I opened the truck door to let some air in, then leaned back and looked out at the road.

GPS. GPS wasn't better than a map. But I didn't want to think about that.

What else? Cell phones? No, cell phones seemed like a good invention to me. A cell phone wouldn't have helped us out here, Dad said. That was probably true. We wouldn't have gotten a signal, and I read once about a woman who got turned around in the woods and went farther and farther off the trail, trying to find a cell signal until she was truly lost. They found all her unsent messages on the phone, and the little camp where she'd starved to death trying to get a cell phone signal. Still, I wouldn't have minded having one. Mom and Dad said when I got my own job and could pay for it by myself, that's when I could get one. For themselves, what did they need with a cell phone, is what they said. A regular phone was bad enough.

Record albums. What was wrong with them? Turntables. My neighbor, Duncan, said the sound was better than anything digital, though I couldn't really tell the difference.

When I was eleven I was walking home from school one afternoon when I felt something hit me on the back of the head. I usually walked home from school alone, because I waited with Carly for her mother to pick her up. The bus didn't run up there where they lived, and Carly's mom had to work until 4:30, so we hung out at the school, fooling around with the recorders and xylophones and drums in the band room, or if it was nice out, hanging upside down on the monkey bars until our heads spun. Or we had swinging contests, seeing who could go the highest without chickening out. When we got braver, we jumped from the swing just as it reached its highest point and we rolled like parachute jumpers in the wood shavings.

Anyway, the hit to the back of my head wasn't hard. It was like a bee had flown into my hair. I kept walking, and then I felt it again. I looked behind me and there were three boys walking down the sidewalk, but they were talking to each other and didn't seem to notice me. Then I felt it again. This time, a balled-up piece of tinfoil from a chocolate bar landed on the sidewalk in front of me. One of the boys said, just loud enough for me to hear, "What's red, white and peeling? A ginger trying to tan."

"What's the difference between a ginger and a vampire? One's pale and blood-sucking and avoids the sun. The other is a vampire."

I tried to walk faster, but the boys kept up to me. I don't know if you've ever noticed that boys like that have this ability that horses are supposed to have—they can sense your fear. Anyway, these boys could, I think. Even though I didn't turn around. Even though I kept walking. When I crossed the street, they crossed too.

One of them started to bark, like an angry little poodle. The other two started, too. I don't know what kind of dogs they were supposed to sound like—bigger ones, anyway.

From my left side, I felt a moving shadow fall across the sidewalk. I jumped and turned and there was our neighbor, Duncan, on his bike. He didn't say anything. He rode slowly along beside me for a couple minutes, standing on his pedals, until the boys, who were younger than him, stopped barking. Then he sped up and kept going. Our lane was just ahead. I always went down the back lane to get home and so did Duncan. When I turned, the boys didn't follow.

At the house, I unlatched the gate.

"Hey!" Duncan called. He was standing in his garage, his backpack on the old couch they had in there, and his drumsticks in his hand. "What're you doing?"

"Nothing. I'm going in the house."

"Your folks home yet?"

"No, not yet."

"C'mhere."

So I went in the garage as he squeezed behind his drum kit and sat down.

"You can sit there if you want." He gestured to the couch. I moved his backpack and sat down. He tapped his sticks together a few times, made a kind of jump on his stool and lit into his drums like he was on fire. He went on like that, lifting off his seat, his mouth twisting and his head going back and forth with the rhythm for about ten minutes.

"Holy! What was that?" I said when he stopped.

"'Sing, Sing, Sing.' I'll play you the record. Drummer named Gene Krupa. Guy was a genius drummer." He stood up and pulled a record down from a shelf, put it on a turntable set up on the workbench behind him.

"Where'd you get the records?" I asked.

"Th-th-th . . . th-th-th . . ." He closed his eyes. Sometimes when I asked Duncan something, I wished I hadn't, because I didn't want him to feel the way I did when I froze. Then he said, "They were my grandpa's. He was a drummer, too."

He put the needle down carefully and we listened to the song and every once in a while, Duncan mimicked the drum part in the air but didn't play it. When it was done, he lifted the needle off the record and said, "I'm going to go in now."

I took my backpack and crossed the lane to our house. I let myself in and as I made myself a peanut butter sandwich, I thought that that was the nicest thing a boy had ever done for me, except for Dad. I knew he had called me in there just to make sure I was okay, and I realized too that I *was* okay. I felt better, like I was someone other than just the scared skinny redheaded girl I'd been on the sidewalk with the boys barking at me.

Disadvantage to being a redhead: it gives jerks an easy thing to tease you about. Advantage to being a redhead: I'll let you know when I think of something. Carly claims she wishes she had red hair, but that's only because she doesn't have red hair.

Since then, Duncan has called me into the garage a few times to listen to things. I would never catch up to him to walk home from school, or even say hi to him away from the garage, because he's usually with a bunch of his band friends and I figure he wouldn't appreciate being seen talking to a girl my age. But that didn't matter. What mattered was that he saw me.

CHAPTER SEVENTEEN

That night I slept with one eye on the sky. I found the Big Dipper and followed its curved handle to bright Arcturus, at the bottom of Boötes. Next to it, I picked out the seven stars in the necklace of the Corona Borealis. I could be in my own yard at home, looking at these same stars. Once in a while my eye caught the streaking of a meteor and by the time I registered what it was, it had melted into the throng of stars.

The red and white lights of an aircraft blinked across the sky. I watched them and sometimes the sound carried all the way down to me by my fire in the fir-branch lean-to. I was thinking how impossible it was that anybody on one of those airplanes could be thinking about me, or someone like me, or someplace like the place where I was, when they were up there, surrounded by artificial light and TV screens and little plastic trays of food. I was on an airplane once with Mom and Phoebe, to go to Ontario when Grandpa Fox died. That was Dad's dad; he was already there. Mom said I could sit beside Phoebe, who was in the seat by the window, but Phoebe said, "No. I don't want her here." Mom tried to argue with her, but there were people in the aisle waiting to get past and so Mom sat down beside Phoebe and I sat in a seat next to a stranger. She was nice anyway, a pretty girl who smelled like oranges and who gave me a little bag of grapefruit jellybeans.

Midway through the flight, Phoebe decided she wanted to switch seats with me, so she got the pretty girl and I got the window and Mom. I'd looked down and seen the shimmer of towns tucked into mountain passes and trails of car lights moving like ant highways and sometimes a lonely point of light in a sea of dark. Maybe someone did look down from that airplane window and see the glow of light my fire cast in all the darkness and maybe they wondered who was there.

The disappearing deer bones kept me awake for a while. A coyote or a wolf or a cougar could have carried them off. Maybe a different animal than the one that killed the deer in the first place. Maybe an eagle or ravens. There was no meanness to it. Whatever it was, I realized, it wasn't trying to scare me. It wasn't going to chase me down just for fun. Whatever it was, it was just like me, trying to survive.

Eventually, I closed both eyes and slept.

I didn't want it to be the first thing in my head when I woke up. It'd been a thing I'd kept to the back of my mind, hovering like a mosquito in my room at night that I try to ignore, but that keeps ending up right by my ear no matter how much I swat at it. But there it was, smack in the front of my mind, first thing: Day Eight is Rescue Day. I know I said I had a rule—no more dreaming of rescue. And I know I hadn't been very good at obeying it. Well, a rule is more of a goal, was the way I saw it. Something to aim for. And now it didn't matter anyway because Day Eight was Rescue Day. Today, instead, the rule was to not think about not-rescue.

I didn't need to rush to get up. Strangely, I was still not very hungry. I looked forward to my breakfast, but only because the tea would be hot and soothing. My Scotch mints were not going anywhere and also, it was still cold. It had been a clear night and the morning dew lay frosty on the grass and road and truck. I dug my matches from my pocket where I kept them to stay dry. I still had plenty, but I would not need plenty. Today, I could stop thinking that way.

What if she walked right out and never turned back?

Once, when we were camping, when Phoebe was still alive, we'd gone to bed in the tent in our usual way—Dad, who was snoring already, and next to him, Mom, then Phoebe next to her, also snoring in her light, bird-whistle way, then me. It was always me on the outside next to the tent wall. It had been deep dark and I'd been lying there listening to the night noises when a twig snapped loudly, close to the tent.

"Why does Phoebe always get to sleep beside you?" I whispered to Mom.

"I don't have to worry about you," Mom said. "You're never afraid."

"Yes I am," I said.

"Oh, Francie. You should be proud of that."

At first I was angry. But after a while I'd started to cry

because it wasn't fair I should be punished for not being afraid. I half-hoped Mom would hear me.

She didn't. She was already asleep.

She could walk out to the road and she would never have to worry about me again.

I gave my head a shake. This was not the kind of thought to have on Rescue Day. It was what I'd just said I would not think. Instead, I worked on building my morning fire.

When the sun came over the treetops and began to warm up the day, I shrugged off my sleeping bag, gave my hands one more warming turn at the fire and went to gather more fir needles for my tea. That done, I chopped the needles with my jackknife and put the water on the little burner to boil. It would be another warm day; I could feel it coming in the air.

I didn't like to just gobble down my breakfast of Scotch mints like I was swallowing vitamins. I made a little ritual of it, setting them out on a bark plate. I took a sip of tea and let it warm my insides. Then I took a mint off the plate and placed it on my tongue. It dissolved slowly. When the last of the sweetness had disappeared, I took a couple more sips of tea. A bald eagle wheeled overhead, tightening his circle. I was sure he saw me, was coming in for a closer look. I took another mint, placed it on my tongue.

Normally, I didn't even like Scotch mints. I used to think they tasted like chalk, or what chalk would taste like if I had ever eaten it, which I hadn't. I'd wondered how they could be Mom's favorite candy. She also likes Rockets, the ones you get in rolls at Halloween. She buys a big bag and eats them for months afterward. Also chalky.

But now, I couldn't believe how delicious the mints were, and how I'd never noticed. The way they melted softly with a tiny sweet fizz and the sugar became almost like icing.

I ate another one. Then another, right from the bag, skipping the ritual. I think I had six or seven before I started to feel a little bit sick. As I twisted the bag closed, I realized something. Just because Mom had left the Scotch mints behind didn't mean she'd left them for me. It didn't mean anything. She'd also left the flashlight behind, her backpack, her sleeping bag, her warm clothes. She'd left everything behind.

What about her purse? Mom had brought her purse with her on this trip. She'd planned to leave it at home, because she said she'd just need to leave it in the truck for the hike, but at the last minute, she'd grabbed it. It was a black, soft-leather satchel like a horse's feed bag. She sometimes called it the Black Hole, because when she put something in there, it was like dropping it into outer space. Even she didn't know what was in there.

I took the bag of mints back to the truck and put them on the dashboard where they wouldn't get accidentally spilled or eaten by mice. I checked the floor and the backseat and under the seats. Mom's purse wasn't there. I'd last seen it—when? It'd been on her shoulder when we went in the gas station to use the bathroom. I bent and stuck my hand under the passenger seat and my fingers touched something soft. It was wedged under there, stuck. I had to use both hands to pull it free.

I unzipped it, the leathery, dried-orange-peel, spearmint-gum smell wafting out. Her wallet, balled up Kleenex, several tubes of lip balm, different flavors, pens and pencils, sticky with lint, twelve of them altogether, two lipsticks, safety pins, bobby pins, hair elastics, a Cover Girl compact smudged with orange powder, a pair of sunglasses, another pair of sunglasses with one of the arms broken, several crinkled and faded receipts, a piece of gum, out of the wrapper and also sticky with lint, which I put in my pocket, a Midas Muffler keychain with no keys on it, a yellow sticky note with a list in her handwriting that said *milk carrots toothpaste tea*, three loose keys, one of those pocket calendars with a picture of a kitten on it. Dad and I had given it to her in her stocking two Christmases ago. The pages were all empty. And three plastic pill bottles, all empty.

I looked at the labels. The prescriptions had Mom's name on them, Adele Fox, but on each one, part of the label had been neatly crossed out with a black felt marker. Who would have done that? And why?

That made me think of her special tobacco, and I knew. I knew like I knew the whining in my gut that Mom had taken her special tobacco with her. She had not taken her flashlight or her Scotch mints or her sleeping bag. She had not taken me. But she'd taken her tobacco.

My mind went down and down in a deep black hole like Mom's purse and it took all my effort to pull it back up to the light of day.

Rescue Day. I had to keep busy.

I left Mom's purse on the floor of the truck. It was warm enough to put on a T-shirt, so I got mine from my pack, and then

I hiked into the woods looking for the perfect stick. I wanted a souvenir of this place, a walking stick I'd carve my initials into and someday when I was grown up, I'd give it to my child and tell him or her the story of my seven days on this road to nowhere.

I picked my way along through the trees, leaves crunching under my footsteps, sun on my shoulders. Every once in a while, I stopped to listen. Once I heard an airplane, lower than a jet, but not that low. Not low enough. No other engine sounds. Just birds peeping and the woodpecker drilling and the crunch of my own feet in the leaves. The day went slowly like that.

I watched some ants soldier along the base of a tree. I watched one drag a stick three times her size across the rusty fir needles. Worker ants are always female; I knew that from my grade-six ant project.

I tried not to, but I heard Mom's scream.

I saw her there in the laundry room standing with the good tablecloth opened out in her two hands and a diamond-shaped hole the size of a paperback book cut out of it.

"Why would you *do* something like that?"

"I didn't."

"Of course you did—don't lie to me on top of it."

She was right. Of course I did it. I'd been doing my ant project at the dining room table, and I'd cut out the cardboard ant with scissors. I must have done it, but I'd pushed aside the tablecloth like she'd told me to and I didn't understand how it happened, so I said again, "I didn't."

Her fingers gripped my arm as she pulled me down the hallway. She held me so hard she shook with it. She didn't mean for it to hurt. It was the only family heirloom we had, the tablecloth. From Ireland, I think. It had been Grandma's. We had the cabin too—that was an heirloom—but we didn't go there anymore and that was my fault, too.

Now I see how my mind went from the ants to the ant project to the tablecloth to the hallway, and I wish I could have stopped it right there, but it was like an ant on its trail back to the nest—it would go over anything to get there. My mind scurried back to my room, always back to my room in the dying-down day, the house silent and breathing with Mom's anger.

"You're going to stay here and give some thought to your actions. That's your problem, Francie. You just don't think about your actions—you're lost in your own dream world."

Which wasn't true at all; I did nothing but think about my actions.

Mom's anger seeped through the vents and filled my room, pinning me to the floor where I lay listening for a peep, a creak, a sign. The sound that came was Dad's boots on the front step, and my heart bubbled a little. Then the front door squeaked open.

"Del! Francie? I'm home."

I sat up, but didn't dare call out. Water running in the bathroom, the toilet flushing. The silence tried to smother these normal sounds; it rushed back in, heavy, thick.

Then low voices. After a while, the smell of onions frying and a clink of silverware. Then voices in the hall:

"Don't you dare go in there." Mom's voice.

"I just want to check on her." Dad's.

"She needs to learn there's consequences."

"It's just a tablecloth, Del. I'm sure it was a mistake."

"Sure. To you it's nothing. Let her blunder through life thinking there is no price to pay. God knows I paid the price."

"So did she. So did she, Del."

And I knew they weren't talking about tablecloths anymore. I didn't hear what Dad said next, but I knew from the soft tone of his voice that he would not be coming to check on me. It would get dark, and it did, and I refused to turn on the light as I lay there on the hard floor listening to the rattle of supper dishes. I pulled my pillow and blanket to the floor, only allowing myself to move that much from where I'd dropped in my despair. When they peeked in at me later, they would see me there and feel sorry.

Then a deep TV voice said, "This is the *National*" and I knew it was time for the ten o'clock news. Dad and the news reporter went on with their routines, not knowing or caring about me lying on the cold floor in the dark. That's when I turned on the light, gathered my blanket and pillow and got into bed. I picked up the book I had been reading, *The Amazing Universe*, and read about Chinese astronomer Yang Wei-Te, who on July 4, 1054, recorded the appearance of a "guest star," a new star so bright he could see it in the daytime for twenty-three days. Today, I read, we can still see the Crab Nebula, which is a cloud of light left over from that exploding star. I turned off my light and looked out my window. I couldn't see it, but I knew it was there.

A faint, faraway rumble brought me back to the stick I'd begun whittling. I looked at my watch. Four o'clock in the afternoon.

I stood to listen to the rumble. It came from the west, the same area where I'd heard the engine rumble the other day. I ran to the truck and hopped up on the tailgate to see if I could spot anything. The sound grew a little louder and then I recognized the *whomp-whomp-whomp* of helicopter blades. I climbed onto the toolbox and used it to boost myself onto the roof.

"Hey!" I yelled, waving my arms madly.

That was useless and I knew it, since the helicopter was nowhere near me yet, but I was so excited that I couldn't help it. It would be just like my fantasy: Mom and Dad jumping down, ducking and running toward me. They knew where I was; they couldn't miss me. A road would not be a hard thing to find in a wilderness of trees.

I hurried to my fire, poked it to life and put on some green boughs, not too many this time. Blue-gray smoke twisted and billowed from it. I climbed back onto the roof of the truck.

The whomp of blades drifted into and out of earshot, like a dream that wouldn't quite become real. At first I stood and waited for it to get closer. I'd wave my arms when it did. After a while, I sat on the roof with my arms around my knees and watched the sun disappear below the trees. As soon as it did, the chill dropped over me.

At six o'clock, I admitted to myself that the sound had faded altogether. At 6:30 I went and built up the fire again. I couldn't make myself eat, if you could call it eating. I knew I'd feel better if I at least had a cup of tea, but I couldn't make myself leave the heat and brightness of the fire and walk into that cold, shadowed dusk.

Where was she? What if she'd gone into the woods to find water, or to pee, and got lost? Where was Dad? Had he ever made it back to the road? If he hadn't, where was he?

Then I had the kind of thought that comes to me at dusk when the sky is the color of dirty dishwater. When Dad was experimenting with the GPS at home, he went through two sets of batteries in one day. He thought he'd figured out why, but he hadn't had a chance to test his theory yet. What if he'd run out of batteries out there? What if he was still walking? If there was one thing Dad was good at, he always said, it was walking.

Leaves crinkled in the undergrowth to the left of me. Something was stepping softly. I felt my heart catch, waiting, and then something let go. All the holding back, all the efforts to keep my mind from rushing to the dark places—it all just let go.

What if Mom was still walking? What if she had not found water? What if she got too tired and stopped walking? What if she had never walked down that road in the first place? What if they were not coming back for me?

Night fell, mild and full of noises. I didn't expect to sleep at all. I forgot to lock the door. I needed to get up and do it. Mom held out the key. I wanted to tell her I didn't need a key to lock the door from the inside, but the words wouldn't come. All the lights had been left on in the living room.

"Look at this place," Dad said. "It's like the Milky Way in here."

I had to lock the door and turn off the lights but I couldn't wake up. *Shuffle, shuffle, shuffle* in the hall outside my room. I struggled to open my eyes. Hands brushing the wall, the fall of heavy footsteps on the carpet, a snap of twigs.

My eyes blinked open. The buzz of deep sleep fogged my brain. Again the snap and crunch of twigs. I held my breath. Something big was moving in the brush not ten feet away. The fire had died out. My fingers searched for the flashlight and closed around it. I switched it on and shone the light toward the brush.

A flashlight! Someone was shining a light back at me.

"Mom!"

Two of them. Two lights.

"Dad? Mom? Who is it?"

My heart lifted, then thudded into my throat. My flashlight beam illuminated a silhouette and I understood. They were not lights. They were eyes. It was a bear. The two eyes caught in my light gazed back at me.

We stared at each other. The bear raised its head and sniffed the air. My mouth was so dry, my heartbeat a wild roar filling my head.

"No," I croaked out.

"No." A little louder. I stood up and made a shooing motion.

"No, bear. Off you go. Off you go, bear." She turned, and in the light I saw that she wasn't big.

"This is my spot," I said, waving again. "Go on now. Leave me alone."

She exhaled a little puff of air and then ducked her head away. With the arc of light from the flashlight, I followed her shape running away from me through the trees. She made a wide circle around me and up onto the road.

Fear fizzed in my ears. I sank back to the ground, my legs quivering. I took deep breaths. I'd done the right thing. I'd stayed calm and talked to her in a low voice. She'd run away, probably as scared as I was. You might think that the first thing I'd do would be to race to the truck with my sleeping bags and shut myself in to spend the rest of the night in there. I admit it was the first thing I thought of. But I made myself stop.

There are bears out here, I told myself, *of course there are. This is the wilderness. This is their home.* I'd surprised the bear by being here. I doubted she would come back. I did not want to get back in that cold, uncomfortable truck. The truth was, I was afraid of the truck. If I got back in the truck, I knew I would not get back out. If no one found me, I'd die of fear in there. Out here, I had my fire, and I could hear if anything was coming.

I dug out my matches and quickly put together a pile of kindling, then lit it. The fire threw comforting heat and light. But also, I thought I'd make sure the bear knew that this was my spot now. Maybe I'd built my camp on one of her usual paths. Maybe she'd seen me and gotten curious. Or maybe she was like me, lost and blundering her way along.

My hand found my water bottle, which I'd stowed beside my sleeping bag. I uncapped it and guzzled most of the water. My mouth was so dry.

What time was it anyway? The broad band of the Milky Way blazed across the sky. The Big Dipper poured the sky from its ladle. I guessed it was about two or three in the morning. What was the bear doing wandering at that time? She was a black bear, I was pretty sure of that, and black bears aren't normally nocturnal.

The last time I saw a bear was in Wild Horse Canyon, and that time, I barely saw it. That was the year I was nine, the second time things went bad for Mom. I'd been waiting for Mom after school because we were supposed to drive up to Kelowna together, have dinner, and then go to an outdoor store that had backpacks for children. The backpack was my birthday present. It wasn't cheap—it was more money than Mom and Dad usually spent for birthdays—so Grandpa and Aunt Sissy had pitched in.

While I waited for Mom, I sat on the school step reading a library book, *The Railway Children*. I guess I'll always remember that as a sad book, because of that day. Maybe it is or maybe it isn't. I don't know. I'll never read it again.

I'd just noticed that I was starting to get cold. It was spring, a nice afternoon, the buds starting to show on the maples and poplars, but I'd been sitting on the concrete step for over an hour. Ms. Fineday came out, just strapping on her bike helmet.

"Hi, Francie!" she said, sounding surprised to see me sitting there. "Good book?"

"Yeah. I'm just waiting for my mom. We're going to Kelowna."

"I saw your mom leaving through the north doors. She was walking."

"Walking? The car's parked out here."

"Maybe she forgot she drove. I do that sometimes."

I had a bad feeling, the kind I get when I'm almost certain something has gone wrong. I kept my voice calm. "I just saw her after class. We said we'd meet here."

Ms. Fineday frowned a little. She wasn't the type who always pretended to know everything. "Maybe she had to run an errand first?"

Tears welled up and clouded my eyes.

"What can I do to help?" Ms. Fineday said kindly.

"I don't know. I think I better wait a little longer."

"Can I wait with you?"

"Sure."

She told me about the climbing she was planning to do at Skaha Bluffs, how she'd been dreaming about a route she'd failed at many times before and she couldn't wait to try it again. She said the hike up to the bluffs was part of the fun, the views were so beautiful, and she said once, she'd nearly sat on a snake.

After about an hour, we went inside and I called home. Mom wasn't there but Dad was. He'd said he'd come and get me and to stay put. Ms. Fineday waited with me until Dad arrived, then Dad and I drove around looking for Mom. We stopped at her favorite cafés and the Indian restaurant where we went for samosas. We drove by the creek where there was a bench she liked to sit on. But she wasn't in any of those places. At about seven o'clock we went home and Dad called the police.

They asked Dad a lot of questions and when he got off the phone, he said, "They said they'll keep their eyes open and to call if she comes home."

At ten o'clock, the phone rang. Dad answered it. It was a teacher from my school, not one of my teachers. He'd seen Mom while he was driving home from badminton and he'd been curious because he noticed her feet were bare. She wouldn't accept a ride, but he told Dad where he'd seen her.

"There you are," she said when we pulled up beside her on Government Street, as if she'd been the one looking for us.

"Where are your shoes?" I said.

"Well, I had to leave the shoes," she said, just in her normal voice, like nothing was weird at all. "I realized the shoes were part of the problem."

"What problem?" I said, but my voice was not normal; it was quivering with all the tears I'd been holding back.

"Never mind, Francie," Dad said. "Let's go home. You must be freezing."

"I'm not too bad," Mom said, even though she was only wearing a jean jacket and no socks or shoes.

It wasn't until the next day that Dad took her to the hospital. She stayed there for the next four months.

I put another branch on the fire. After a few minutes, it caught and flared with warmth. I'd relaxed enough to lie back down, but I kept the sleeping bag away from my face so I could keep my ears open. The sky had begun to lighten a little; I could make out shapes around me, the truck on the road and the trees in the woods on the other side.

My mind had wandered. I'd started to remember the last time I'd seen a bear. Ms. Fineday did an overnight hiking trip every June with ten kids who were twelve and older. At the last minute one of the kids had to cancel and Ms. Fineday managed to convince the principal that I'd be able to keep up with the older kids. Mom was in the hospital then and I knew Ms. Fineday was trying to help out.

It was June and the little creeks were still running. When we crossed the first one, Ms. Fineday said, "We'll cross a couple more of these on our trail and we can fill our water bottles then. That's why we didn't have to carry so much water from home. A liter of water weighs one kilo. Two liters, you're adding two kilos of weight to your pack. That's over four pounds."

The Wild Horse Canyon trail crossed a burned-over area, so it was mostly open, and hot, not a lot of shade. Most of us would go through almost a liter of water in an hour. Even though the temperature was in the high seventies, it felt much hotter out there, with the remains of charred, twisted pines baking in the morning sun.

Another thing I liked about Ms. Fineday was that she didn't pepper me with pointless questions the way other adults did. You know: How are you doing? How are things at home? Are you and your dad managing okay? (As if we were both babies who didn't know how to look after ourselves.) And school? How's school?

Anyhow, Ms. Fineday—whose first name, I found out, is Mary-Jane, not that I'd ever call her that, but that's what Laila, the other adult on our trip, called her—Ms. Fineday didn't stare at me with a sad, disappointed face, as if I'd done something embarrassing.

By the time we reached the campsite on the lake, all of the kids, not just me, were worn out and hungry. Some kids dropped their packs and walked right into the lake with their clothes on. Some of the boys stripped down to their under-wear; they didn't care who saw. We were all laughing crazily, so relieved to dive under the silky cool water.

The air, heavy with the smells of sage and pine, stayed warm and inviting even as the sun set. We swam while Ms. Fineday and Laila made the fire. Then those who wanted to sleep in tents set them up. I hadn't brought a tent, because I didn't have one small enough to carry.

"You can sleep in my tent," Ms. Fineday said. "I don't snore."

"No, thank you," I said. "I want to sleep under the stars."

"It's a sleep-under-the-stars kind of night," she agreed.

I had never slept out in the open, without a tent. It felt wonderful to lie there looking out at the moon on the lake. The warm earth soothed my tired muscles.

Sometime near morning, I heard one of the boys call out, "Ms. Fineday!" Not shouting, but short and sharp.

She unzipped her tent. "What's up, Jeremy?"

"There's something down by the lake. It's something big. It just came through here a minute ago."

My eyes opened. The other kids sleeping outside sat up.

"Yes, I see it. Not to worry. It's a bear getting a drink. She won't bother us."

"There's a cub, too," one of the girls said.

From where I was, I could just see through the trees the dark head of the mother bent to the water.

"I'll just make sure she sees us," Ms. Fineday said, getting out of her tent. "Hey, bear!" she called, in a calm voice. "See us over here? Get your drink and move along."

The bear looked over at her. She didn't seem concerned at all. Laila poked her head out of her tent. "Should I make some noise?"

"We'll give her a minute. She sees us."

A minute or two later, the cub galloped off, heading up the hill, away from us. The mother bear turned and followed.

"Nice morning," Ms. Fineday said. "You can all get some more sleep if you like. I'm going to make coffee."

I stayed in my sleeping bag, listening to Ms. Fineday and Laila by the fire.

Laila said, "I was worried when I saw that cub. You were as cool as a cucumber."

"It's a myth that a black bear with a cub is dangerous," Ms. Fineday said. "A grizzly, yes. But black bear cubs can climb trees, so the mums don't worry too much about them. If she feels threatened, she'll just send her cub up a tree."

"I didn't know that," Laila said.

"There are a lot of myths about bears that people just pass on without knowing if they're true or not. They're not cuddly teddy bears, but they're not vicious killers either. A bear usually wants to stay out of your way as much as you want to stay out of hers."

The smell of coffee had drifted on the fresh morning air. I don't even like coffee, but lying by my own fire now, I remembered that smell as rich and delicious. Another thing Ms. Fineday had told us kids later was that bears don't normally roam the woods at night. Their habits are much like humans, getting up at dawn and bedding down at dusk, unless there are a lot of humans or other disturbances around during the day, which forces them to change their habits. Then they may become nocturnal, looking for food, mostly plants and insects, at night.

That's why I wondered about this little bear. Did it mean there were humans active nearby? Or could it be that she was trying to avoid an older, bigger bear? I decided she was on her own, and scared, and thinking of her that way let me fall asleep again.

CHAPTER EIGHTEEN

I might as well tell you about the shoes. You're probably wondering why Mom was walking all over Penticton without her shoes. Or maybe you're not wondering at all and it's only me who still can't get it out of my head, even though it happened a long time ago.

Aunt Sissy had come to stay. Most of the time, Dad and Aunt Sissy got along. Dad gets along with everyone, Mom always says, and I think it's true. He sees the good in people, no matter what. He always says hello to the neighbors who leave beer bottles on their front lawn. When they play their music too loud on the weekends, Dad'll say, "At least it's Bob Seger," or whoever it is that he likes. In the winter, when Dad's shoveling snow, he shovels in front of their house, too. He says we could have worse neighbors. Mom always smiles at that, and says, "Yes, you're right, we could have worse."

Anyway, when Dad and Aunt Sissy did disagree, it was usually about Mom. Or about why Aunt Sissy had come to stay. Usually, after I'd gone to bed, Dad sat in the living room watching TV and Aunt Sissy went to her room, a room we called the den, that was full of a jumble of different-sized bookcases, a saggy old hideaway bed, a kitchen table that was in Mom's first apartment when she was eighteen and that we used for a desk, and a gooseneck floor lamp. But if Aunt Sissy stayed up to watch the news, I could hear her and Dad talking, because my room was right above the living room.

One of their arguments went like this:

Dad said, "I know you wanted to see Del, but now you've seen her, so I think it's okay for you to go home. Don't you have a law practice to take care of?"

"I'm just staying until things are a little more settled," Aunt Sissy said.

"What things? I can certainly take care of things here. You're the feminist."

"This is what sisters do. You might as well accept it."

"It's not that I don't appreciate it." I could hear Dad's voice softening. "And I know it's nice for Francie to have someone here after school."

"Don't take this the wrong way," Aunt Sissy said and stopped.

(Have you ever noticed that when someone starts a sentence that way, you're almost guaranteed to take it the wrong way?)

"Don't take this the wrong way," she said again. "But I don't think you always get hold of the right end of the stick on this."

"On what?"

"On Del, on what she's going through. I think you indulge her too much. Like the shoes, for instance. Did you even ask her why she'd lost her shoes or did you just go out and buy her a new pair?"

"I don't think she lost them."

137

"Left them, whatever."

"There's no point in asking that kind of thing."

"That's my point!"

I thought to myself that she sounded just like a lawyer then.

Dad was quiet. I could hear the news reporter on TV.

"Well, I asked her," Aunt Sissy went on. "And do you know what she told me?"

"I think you're going to tell me whether I want to hear it or not." Dad laughed a little.

"But why wouldn't you want to hear it? That's what I don't understand."

"No, we don't see eye to eye on that point, that's true, Sis."

(Dad was the only one who called Aunt Sissy "Sis." Mom said it was just like him, finding a middle ground between Sissy and Cecilia.)

Aunt Sissy dropped her voice, but I still heard her perfectly.

"She said her shoes were *listening* to her."

"Okay," said Dad.

"She said they had been bugged. Her plan was to get a new pair, but everything downtown was closed. It was almost comical. I couldn't stop myself from laughing."

"That would upset her."

"Well, yes, it did upset her, but we can't pussyfoot around her delusions."

"You call it pussyfooting around."

"I do. I've spoken with the psychiatrist about it. She agrees with me."

"I just don't want to upset Del. It's hard enough."

"The government bugged her shoes. That's what she said."

138

"Okay, Sis."

"You're putting your head in the sand," Aunt Sissy said.

"Okay." Then he turned up the news and I heard the reporter talking about high-energy biscuits and medical kits arriving in Burma.

I felt sick. I wished I had plugged my ears.

I don't know who was right in that argument, Dad or Aunt Sissy. I've thought about it a lot, but I can't sort it out. Each of them seemed a little bit right and a little bit wrong. What I do know is that it's not nice to be the one who upsets Mom. It's not nice and you don't want to do it, if you can help it.

But it's different for sisters. Sisters can upset each other and nothing can make them not sisters anymore.

Fear has a taste. That's what I was thinking when I woke up in my fir-bough lean-to on the ninth day. I remembered a taste in the back of my throat as I realized the lights shining back at me were not flashlights but eyes. It was a metal taste, or something sharp and silvery like that. I'd had a moment of excitement, relief. I could almost feel Mom's arms around me. And then the sharp taste seared my throat. I could hardly get a word out. What had I said?

No. Off you go, bear. And she had gone. Even now I felt the leftovers of fear, like when I've cried myself to sleep and wake up feeling stiff and stupid.

The sun was high enough to shine in on my face as I sat up, but a cold breeze gusted up the road. Scrambled eggs were the next thing in my mind and when I thought of that, I felt a slip—weariness, helplessness—gaining on me. I almost lay back down. Why not snug the sleeping bag tight, let the sun shine on my face, and just wait? I would be rescued, or not. What difference did it make if I kept on trying to survive?

I went as far as to brush my hand over my sleeping bag to smooth out the lumps. My body leaned to it and then I remembered Ms. Fineday saying to me after the hiking trip, "I'm proud of you, Francie. You're a brave girl."

I straightened myself. I wanted to prove she was right.

CHAPTER NINETEEN

I think I had noticed something out of the corner of my eye even before my mind caught up to it. A patch of moisture soaked into the dirt behind the truck. It had not rained; the rest of the road was dry.

I pulled on my rain jacket against the wind and got up. I saw the cooler first. It lay on its side in the ditch. I went to it and picked it up. It was empty, of course. Two puncture holes pierced its side. How could I not have heard anything? The bucket lay a few feet away, also empty. The little bear had pulled the cooler and bucket down from the truck tailgate where I'd left them and now my water was gone. Had she at least gotten a drink first? I hoped she had. One of us should have had that water.

I was in trouble now. My own water bottle was almost empty. Why hadn't I filled the plastic cube we'd brought to use in camp in the Grand Canyon? I hadn't thought of it. I thought I had more than enough. I didn't expect to need it past Day Seven and now . . . I ran to my lean-to and pulled out my water bottle. There was maybe a quarter of a cup left.

Stupid, stupid.

The still I'd made—I'd forgotten all about it. But when I hurried to it, my heart sank. The plastic had drooped into the center and pulled away from one side. I squatted and carefully peeled the plastic up. An eighth of a cup, maybe, of yellowy water lay in the cooler lid.

Now that I couldn't have it, fir needle tea seemed like the best breakfast I could imagine. Forget scrambled eggs. I longed for that warm, piney cup of tea. My hands around the cup, breathing in the scent.

I had eight Scotch mints left. I ate two, and had to fight myself not to eat the rest. Then I chewed down some dandelion leaves. The inside bark of some trees was edible, I thought. But what trees? My survival book was specific about certain types of trees—hemlock, for example, which shouldn't be confused with other trees. The worst thing I could do out here was eat the wrong thing, give myself stomach cramps or worse. I needed to find water.

First, I went to the truck and emptied my backpack. The plastic cube Dad had bought at Canadian Tire was still folded up in its package. I pulled it open. The package said it could hold twenty liters. Ms. Fineday had said that a liter of water weighs one kilo. So full, the cube would weigh twenty kilos, or about forty-five pounds, more than half my weight. Well, I didn't need it to be full. I knew I could manage twenty pounds or so.

I stuffed the cube in my pack, along with my hoodie and the mints. I got a fresh box of matches and put that and my jackknife in my rain jacket. My compass, paper and a pencil went in the other pocket. I put my sleeping bags in the truck in case it rained. What else? My water bottle, of course. That's all I could think of. I wanted to travel as light as possible, but I knew I still had to be prepared. I hesitated, thinking, then threw in the portable stove, a fuel canister and the pot. I could make myself a nice cup of hot tea as a reward once I found water.

The last thing I did was to take the note Mom had written for us out of the window. I took a fresh sheet of paper from my drawing pad and wrote:

I'm stranded on this road. I've been here nine days. I've gone to look for water. Please wait for me.

Then I added *P.S. I'm thirteen years old.*

As I set the note on the dashboard, my hand trembled, then my lip. For a moment I saw myself from outside, a small, pathetic girl, hungry, thirsty, eighty-five pounds soaking wet, probably more like eighty now. Sun streamed down on my lean-to and I longed to curl up there, protected from the cold wind.

A flicker of movement caught my eye. There, on the road in front of the truck, a few feet away, was a little red fox. It sat calmly in the sun, bright black eyes snapping. The bottom part of its front legs was black. White fur fanned out like a mask from its black-tipped nose and ran down its throat and belly. The color of the rest of its soft-looking fur was almost like the color of my hair, a red too red to be strawberry blonde. But it shimmered beautifully in the morning sun and quivered in the wind. It took my breath away. I decided she was a she; a smile loosened the tension I didn't know I'd been holding in my mouth. I stood very still. I wasn't sure if she'd seen me; the truck door hid my body. Then she turned her little head and her black eyes met mine. She seemed to say, "What are you waiting for?"

She stood and tiptoed softly off down the road. South. The same direction the elk had gone. What was this road leading all the animals to? Deer came to the edge of Gem Lake at dawn and dusk to drink. The elk I'd seen at dawn on the road must have either come from a water source, or been heading to one. Maybe the fox was looking for water, too.

I hefted my pack, and followed.

I kept my eyes on her as she slipped into the woods where the road ran out. She cleared logs and deked through the brush easily. I hurried to keep up.

She skipped on, twenty or more yards ahead of me, but she didn't seem to be in a hurry. She stopped and sat in the sun pouring into a clearing, turned her face to it, just like I would. She seemed to be listening. I moved quietly ahead and then stopped, too, watching the swish of her bushy tail, her sharp ears turning to catch the sounds of the forest. She knew I was there, I thought, but she didn't seem to mind.

Except for a crow squawking and the wind moaning through the treetops, the forest was quiet. I held my breath. A tree creaked like a door swinging on rusty hinges. The fox turned her face toward me and then she was up and traveling again, tiptoe, tiptoe, a little bounce in her step. I followed.

I thought I could almost make out a path she was moving along, over downed trees but skirting the thickest underbrush. I caught just enough glimpses of movement to stay on her trail.

"Ready or not here I come." My voice called out to Phoebe. I thought I saw the flicker of her hair in the sunlight.

"You can't catch me."

The emerald green of the lake shone beyond the trees. I ran

for the lawn, my heart pounding. A moment to think she was fast, I never knew Phoebe could run that fast, then a shadow of worry. Mom would be mad. I was not supposed to chase Phoebe; she was not supposed to run all out like that.

I reached the lawn. A hummingbird darted from the feeder near the porch, its wings a buzz, and was gone. I'd lost her. A clamor of voices—mine, Mom's, Grandma's. I stopped in my tracks.

The tree creaked in the wind, *squeak*, *squeak*, swinging on its sticky hinge. I'd lost her. The fox had melted into the woods. A ghost of a trail seemed to wind through the underbrush, but I wasn't sure. I felt like I'd been traveling in a straight line, moving south, but of course that probably wasn't true. And then I realized that I'd completely forgotten to use my compass. I'd followed a fox to who-knows-where. How long had I even been walking? I hadn't checked the time. I hadn't looked behind me. I'd done everything wrong. Like a stupid kid.

Stay found. That's the rule for not getting lost. Keep track of where you are. I had not done that.

Don't panic. Don't plunge on wildly. That's the worst mistake I could make now.

I squatted in the dirt and took out my compass. I knew the road ran north to south. I thought I'd been traveling south and that I'd kept my back to the north. But when the compass needle stopped moving, I saw I'd done what almost every other traveler does who isn't paying attention. I'd veered far off course.

What my instinct told me was north, toward the truck, was actually west. Without noticing, I had strayed to the east, rather than keeping south. I looked at my watch. But that was impossible. Five after two. How could that be? Had I checked my watch when I first got up? No. I had guessed the time was about ten, but I hadn't checked. Could I have really slept past noon? Or could I have zoned out following the fox for much longer than I thought?

I shrugged off my backpack and leaned it against a tree. Then I walked about five feet out and took another compass reading, just in case something had thrown off the first reading. But it was the same. I was somewhere east and south of the truck, no closer to knowing where water lay.

I would not let myself think "lost," not yet. I sat down again. I had to decide what to do. I could try to find my way back to the truck from here. I'd still be without water, no way to have something warm in my stomach, which had been so comforting each morning. Or I could continue looking for water and then find my way back from there.

There was that ridge to the east more or less parallel to the road that could extend this far. Or it might not. Trying to find it would mean straying even farther away from the road than I already was. That would be risky. Who was I kidding? Anything I could do now would be risky. Not finding water was risky, too. Under normal conditions, a person could survive a few days without water. But these weren't normal conditions. I felt pretty good, maybe a little light-headed sometimes, a little shaky too. I wasn't sure what would be causing that, other than being deprived of food. My pants seemed a little looser than normal, but that could be my imagination.

A gust of wind swept through the forest, tossing the branches and bending smaller trees. Then the eerie *creak*, *creak*. Shivering grass and brush rustled like a bubbling stream.

I made up my mind. I would mark the spot where I was now and walk out in one-minute sections, using the compass. I was determined to find water before I returned to the truck.

First, I took out my paper and pencil and drew a rough map of where I thought the road and the truck were. Then I marked in the directions the compass showed and where I thought I was now. I drew in the position of the ridge and where I'd found the deer bones. I added my lean-to and my firepit and under them, I wrote "home." Funny how cozy it seemed now, the fragrant lean-to next to my firepit, the truck with my supplies in it.

I carefully folded the map and put it back in my raincoat pocket. The next thing I needed to do was mark this spot. I hadn't retrieved my fluorescent T-shirt from the ridge trail marker and I hadn't brought anything extra with me. I could use my yellow rain jacket, but the wind had picked up and I didn't think it would be a good idea to get chilled. Also, if I made a miscalculation, which was always possible, then I'd be out in the cold woods overnight without my jacket.

Anything bright that wouldn't blend into the forest colors would be helpful. I dug through my backpack. The pack itself was a dull blue. But inside it, there was a special compartment for a sleeping bag and the cloth used for it was red. The backpack was what Mom called my "most treasured possession." I didn't want to wreck it. But that was silly. I needed to do whatever it took to survive.

I unfolded my jackknife and poked a hole in the red pocket fabric. Then I carefully cut out a square about ten inches by ten inches. It would do. It would stand out against the greens and browns of the woods.

Next, I gathered two long branches. One, I set firmly against a living tree, resting on its lower branches and with the bottom out at a forty-five-degree angle. Then I leaned the other branch against that at the opposite angle so that the bottom of it was snugged against the trunk of the same tree. It made a large X next to the tree. A third, smaller branch I wedged into the soft forest floor and braced the X with it so it wouldn't fall over. I tested it by giving it a shake. It seemed secure enough to hold up against the wind gusts that were rising now more often and rushing through the woods.

I made a hole in the red fabric and stuck it on the end of the X that extended out from the tree. That was my flag to guide me back to this spot, since my walks out and back using my compass readings wouldn't be precise. If you're left-handed, you veer left. If you're right-handed you'll veer right. Apparently even when people know that, they still assume it applies only to other people, with poor senses of direction, not to themselves. They can still be convinced they're walking in a straight line. I've even read that people who think they have a good sense of direction are *more* likely to get lost, not less. They're less likely to pay proper attention.

Well, I would be super-careful. I would keep track of my progress and write it on my map. I was still not ready to call myself lost. I was just temporarily off-track. The road couldn't be far from this X. Once I found water, I'd find the road.

I took out my compass and found south. I needed some kind of landmark to walk toward. The forest looked like an unbroken line of lichen-draped firs and straight gray-black trunks. But the longer I stood looking, the more things started to distinguish themselves. One of the trees was fuller, with starry-looking clusters of needles and a pointy top. It was not a fir, maybe a larch, or what Grandma used to call a tamarack. I'd aim for that one. It was a little off south at 190 degrees, but as long as I kept track, it would work.

"Trust the tools," Dad sometimes said when he was working on his car. If you use a tool the way it was meant to be used, it will work.

My return direction would be ten degrees. I wrote it down on my map, looked at my watch, and began walking. You can walk farther in one minute than you might think. After thirty seconds I'd already stumbled into some fairly thick brush. I had to fight my way through. I was glad to be walking again, because the wind was cold and, standing still, I'd cooled down.

After one minute, I looked around and listened. The creaking tree had a different sound now in the stronger wind—a long, drawn out single *creeeak*, before it relented and creaked back the other way. The rushing wind sounded more like rushing water, a sound I remembered from Gem Lake when the wind came up and traveled through the treetops, but didn't move much on the ground. We always thought it sounded like a waterfall.

Other than that, the landscape seemed the same. I checked the compass at 190 degrees and walked toward the tree with the pointy top. I followed this pattern for five one-minute periods of walking, marking each on my map. Though I was wearing pants, my legs were getting poked from fighting my way through undergrowth. My arms were better protected with my raincoat, but sharp branches caught on my sleeves too.

When I looked behind, I couldn't see my flag, but that was okay. I'd find it when I retraced my steps. This time, when I looked around, I did notice something new: a patch of dark-green plants with tiny, white star-shaped flowers. The flowers weren't familiar to me, but the pairs of deep-green leaves were. They looked like Solomon's seal.

I walked another minute, ducking under a huge tree that had fallen and landed at about my neck height and caught on a broken stump a few yards away. It looked fresh-fallen. The stump was off my southern path, but its reddish bark looked like it could hold something to eat. In my rising fear when I first realized I'd gone off course, I'd forgotten hunger for a while, but now it had returned more powerful than before. My stomach cried out for something warm and filling.

I couldn't lose my path here, I reasoned. I'd just follow the fallen tree to the stump, then return to the same spot. Simple. But I was still nervous. Just to be extra sure, I slipped my arms out of my pack and left it in my path under the fallen tree. When I got to the stump, I checked around its base. Sure enough, large black ants were busily moving around it and up the side. Were all ants edible? I'd never heard of a poisonous ant.

I watched them for a couple of minutes. Then I plucked one off the stump. I looked at it squirming between my thumb and forefinger.

"Sorry, buddy," I said, squished it and popped it into my mouth.

It wasn't too bad. Sort of sour, like vinegar on french fries. I plucked off another and ate it. They'd be better fried, I thought, with some salt. Anything was better with salt. I remembered the salty sunflower seeds I'd finished. French fries from the Jeffer's truck that parked on Nanaimo Avenue in downtown Penticton. Sometimes Dad surprised Mom and me by bringing home a big paper cup of them, glistening with salt.

The ants, I noticed, were all making their way up the trunk, or back down again. The nest must be in the top. I wanted to get up there and have a look. I could walk along the downed tree, but especially with the wind the way it was, it would be dangerous. That thought led to another. Was it going to storm? I looked up at the small piece of sky I could see. Still that bright sky-blue, still sunny, but clouds were scudding across in places. At home, it could blow hard all afternoon and then drop to dead calm as soon as the sun went down. Sometimes Mom and I sat on the patio and watched it happen, the leaves of the maple suddenly going still.

Anyway, I figured I'd better hurry. I probably only had two or three hours of light left. I found a stout log nearby and lifted one end of it, then pushed it over so that it hit the big stump. With a little more maneuvering, I managed to position it to give me a boost that allowed me to scramble up to the top of the stump.

I'd never been so happy to see ants, a teeming nest of them and some fat white larvae. These I scooped with a piece of bark and stuck in my rain jacket pocket. I squished and ate some more ants, shuddering a bit at the sour taste. Then I scooped more onto the bark. They swarmed over my hand and up my jacket sleeve. I fought to stay focused. I found another piece of bark and sandwiched the two together, squishing quite a few in one go. Then I shook off my hand and brushed the others off my sleeve. I'd save this bunch and try cooking them with the larvae tonight when I got back to camp. For now, I made sure they were all dead and shook them into my pocket.

Then I hurried back to my pack. It was time to get moving. As I took my compass reading, I noticed something else. Some new trees had come into view to the left of the pointy treetop. They were tall, deciduous trees, a stand of them. That was a good sign. That could mean water.

No sooner had I noticed the stand of trees tossing in the wind than some other things began to appear: ferns I hadn't noticed before poking through the soil, a blanket of tiny blue flowers with vivid green foliage, the maple-shaped leaves of a thimbleberry bush. I clocked off my minute of walking, ticked it off on my map and then I was sure of what I hadn't wanted to allow myself to believe; the rushing sound I heard was not just wind. I distinctly heard the babble of water running over rocks.

Stay calm; stay focused. One more minute at 190 degrees and then I saw it. Another thirty seconds and I was looking down into a clear, green stream. In places, it stretched ten or fifteen yards across. To my right, west, the creek widened and burbled softly over a field of rocks, beyond which was a narrowed passage that seemed to curve, in which direction I couldn't tell. To my left, east, the creek was faster and narrower, frothing up around rocks scattered across it. I marked a tree with my knife so I'd know where to take the compass reading on the way back.

There was a steep bank down to the creek, but the roots of big trees were exposed and formed natural steps that I used to pick my way down. I filled my water bottle, dropped in one of the purification tablets we'd brought for our hike and shook the bottle to dissolve it. I needed to wait thirty minutes before it was safe to drink. I was so tempted to gulp the fresh, cold water just as it was, but I had to be smart. It looked clean, crystal clear, but a dead animal could be rotting in the water farther upstream and I'd never know it. I had to wait.

I knelt and washed my face and neck. Was this a creek or a river? Would it be on our Oregon road map? I'd left that map in the truck. I dried my hands on my pants and took out my own map, drew in the creek, trying to make it to scale. As I drew, I noticed something: my pencil wasn't casting a shadow on the paper, as it had earlier.

I looked up. Clouds had gathered and darkened to a threatening gray. At the moment I digested that thought, a powerful gust of wind blasted through the forest, churning the branches of the tall trees along the creek. Something snapped and crashed down in the woods above the bank. I'd better fill the bladder and get back to the truck. Then another blast, roaring like an oncoming train. I ducked lower against the creek bank and watched the wind rip off branches and cartwheel them above the water.

I got out the plastic water cube and crouched by the creek, holding the mouth of the container under the water. I'd boil this later. I gazed upstream. If I followed the stream that way, it was possible I could run into the ridge, head north, and eventually come across my fluorescent orange T-shirt, then follow the trail back to the truck. But if the ridge didn't extend this far, I'd be in for a long walk. And what if I came to a ridge, but it was the wrong one? I squinted into the distance. Something caught my eye, lying beside the creek—a shock of red in a landscape of gray stones, brown mud and green leaves.

I quickly screwed the lid on the water cube and laid it next to my pack. The red thing lay about twenty yards off, upstream on the muddy shore close to the water. I had to pick my way over rocks and tree roots in places.

As I got closer, I saw blue. My heartbeat caught and began to quicken. I knew what it was. I stumbled over slippery rocks and there it was, just as if he'd dropped it and would be back— Dad's Canada Post toque. I picked it up, my heart hammering. It was clean and dry.

"Dad!" I screamed. Where was my whistle? "Dad!" Louder. I turned and screamed north, into the wind, then west, east, and south again. And again. The wind bore down on me, roaring then dropping, then rising again and tearing branches from trees. The first spits of rain peppered my jacket.

I checked my watch: 4:15 p.m. It told me what my mind didn't want to accept: I had run out of time. I could not try to find my way back to the truck this late or in this storm. It would be stupid. I thought of my warm shelter, my three sleeping bags dry in the truck, my fire. I could sleep in the truck tonight if I went back. I'd be safe from the storm at least. I turned over Dad's hat in my hands.

"What should I do?" I cried out loud.

"Dad!" I shrieked again. The edge of panic, the fear was in my voice. I could cross the creek here. He could be just ahead. *Calm down. Hunker down.* It was what he would say: "Hunker down, Squirt." I needed to put thoughts of my "home" camp out of my head. I pulled on his toque and tugged it over my ears. I needed to find another shelter.

CHAPTER TWENTY

With the storm blotting out what was left of the day, darkness was falling fast. The wind had risen to a continuous moaning whistle high in the trees. The gloomy woods rang with creaks and snaps and rushes. I scrambled over the rocks and roots back to my pack. Digging through it, I pulled out the whistle. I gave three long blasts on it in each direction. My hands shook, with cold or fear or hunger, or all three.

Where to make my camp? I walked down the bank to the west, where the creek slowed and widened. Giant, gnarled tree roots had made a kind of cave in the bank. I followed the roots up. It was a huge cedar and it had been there a long time. The deciduous trees were bending crazily in the wind, but this cedar seemed like it would hold its own. I had no time to be picky. It was almost dark.

A large rock anchored the tree roots on the east corner. The creekbank would shield me from the worst of the north wind. I crouched down into it to try it out. Immediately I felt warmer, protected. I climbed the roots back up to the woods. There I was met with icy blasts of wind and rain. My flashlight was in my pack, but it wasn't hard to find good-sized limbs to use for my shelter. The wind had strewn them across the forest floor. When I picked one up, the wind tried to rip it from my hands. It nearly knocked me over.

One by one, I dragged several large branches to the edge of the bank, then threw them over onto the shore. Then I scrambled back down to where I'd be spending the long night. No blankets, no food, no company. But I could make hot tea. That would have to be enough.

A night not fit for man nor beast. Dad used to say that when he came home from work on a blustery winter afternoon. I always thought it was funny, because he'd walked all day in it. He'd tromped up sidewalks that hadn't been shoveled and pried open screen doors that were blocked by snow. He'd stepped carefully on ice and poked envelopes into slots and tried not to be scared of dogs snarling at the ends of their chains.

His wool toque was pulled low over my forehead and ears. I'd been instantly warmer when I put it on; it was like he'd left it for me. There was no way that was true, but it made me feel better. My fire sparked and twisted in the wind. I hoped I hadn't built it too close to my shelter. I was comfortable enough, cross-legged on a springy bed of fir limbs, with others pulled in around me to protect me from the worst of the cold. My back was against my pack. I had my hands around the small pot of tea. I'd forgotten the tin cup, but the pot worked well enough. On my knee lay two mints, which I planned to savor once I'd finished the tea. Through the opening I'd left to watch and tend the fire, I could see a slice of the creek, lit by firelight and pitted with rain.

Where was Dad? Was he close by, close enough to see my fire? He must have dropped the hat, but when? Was it on the day he'd first set out walking? If it was, he was far off a southern course, even farther than I had been when I discovered my error today. I pushed away my next thought, barely formed: Dad was left-handed. He'd veered left. But that didn't make sense, because he had the GPS. At least at the beginning of his walk, it should have been functioning. As long as he checked it, he should have been able to stay on course.

As long as he checked it.

The other possibility was that he'd dropped the hat on his way back, looking for the road and the truck. What were the chances we'd crossed paths? What were the chances he was at the truck right now? I felt sick to think of it. My head buzzed and I leaned farther back against my pack to steady myself. It must be hunger.

Then I remembered the ants and larvae I'd stuffed in my jacket pocket. I'd have to fire up the stove again to fry them. I fished them from my pocket and looked at them lying in my hand. Then I popped them into my mouth raw instead and quickly washed them down with a gulp of warm tea.

Where was Mom? Could she still be out in this? She had no knife, no supplies of any kind. She must have reached the road. For some reason, she wasn't able to get back to me. But she'd said she would and I believed her. She said to wait for her. Maybe she'd fallen and hit her head on a rock.

I would not think of that. Instead, I suddenly felt Phoebe near me. The way her hand felt in mine, warm, always a bit sweaty. I felt her nestled next to me, her head on my shoulder and her happy laugh. When we used to sit on the couch together watching TV, she always dug her feet under my legs to keep them warm. Sometimes we brought the blankets off our beds and made a tent of them. Phoebe usually fell asleep in there and I had to try to pull myself out without waking her up.

I ate my mints, sucking every last crystal of sweetness from them. The gnarled piece of root I'd put on my fire had burned through. I pulled another section onto the flame, leaned back to watch it catch. The storm raged above me, a night not fit for man nor beast. I stretched my legs out to try to warm my toes without setting my boots on fire.

I don't remember lying down. A thunderous crash woke me. I sat up. The fire smoldered. Somewhere close, a big tree had fallen, making the ground shudder. I was cold, especially my legs, which had only one layer of protection, and my feet. I found my poking stick and dragged another piece of wood onto the fire, then poked it and blew on it till it flared back to life.

Flicking on my flashlight, I swept the beam across the creek and up along the shore. It had stopped raining. I thought I saw movement down by the wide, slow part of the creek. I shone the beam in that direction, but it was hard to see. Maybe that dark bulk near the water was something. But with the wind churning everything into motion, it was hard to tell. I withdrew back into my cave and tried to warm my feet and legs.

What if it was Dad down by the creek? What if he was weak and crawling?

That was a stupid thought. That was my imagination getting carried away.

Part of me wanted to get out of the cave and run down the shore. Another part wanted to lie down, squeeze my eyes shut and pray for morning. If the shape were an animal—a bear, or a wolf—would the fire keep it away? *They're just trying to survive like I am*, I reminded myself. *They've got no reason to bother me.*

Under the moan of the wind, I thought I heard something else—a cry. It sent chills up my spine. An owl or a coyote? I leaned out into the wind and listened. As the wind relented to gather itself, the air rang with a blood-curdling scream that sounded like something being tortured. I jumped in fear and dropped my flashlight, watched it roll into the fire before I could catch it.

I grabbed my poking stick and tried to fish the flashlight out. Sparks flew up in the night as I fumbled for it. Some landed on the boughs inside my shelter. The flashlight rolled deeper into the nest of flames. I could barely see it.

Be careful now. My stick pushed some red-hot coals aside. I tried to roll the flashlight toward me, without flicking hot embers onto myself or my highly flammable bed of fir boughs. *That was a bad idea*, I thought. *Roll it to the side.*

The crazed scream came again, close by. I felt the tears rising. With a strong flick of my wrist, the flashlight finally bounced out of the fire, landed on a rock and rolled away into the mud of the shore. It was safe now. I would let it cool. I should get it before morning, before the dew or more rain came. I wanted light, but even more I wanted not to set foot out of the safety of my cave.

My ears strained for sounds of movement, something creeping nearer or another scream, but anything I might have heard was drowned out by the blood pounding in my ears. I leaned out again. I couldn't see far—an orange glow of firelight reflected on the water, the gloom of shoreline.

It was not human, I told myself. There was no way it was human. It was animal, some animal I'd never heard before.

Suddenly, I was struck with the powerful sense that I'd made a big mistake in leaving the safety of the truck. Stay put; that's the rule when you're lost. Stay put. I should have stayed put. I could be wrapped in warm sleeping bags right now, inside our trusty old Mazda, safe from the storm—a windshield and steel between me and whatever those noises were.

I couldn't possibly sleep. I lay half on my backpack staring at the fire. Once in a while I sat up, pulled another branch onto the flames. Then I lay back with my ears alert, my heartbeat roaring. Finally, I couldn't stand the listening and waiting to hear that scream again, so I tore corners of paper off my map, wadded them up and stuffed them in my ears. All I could hear now was my own blood rushing furiously.

I drew closer to the fire and checked my watch by its light. It was only 12:30 a.m. I couldn't believe it. I still had at least another six hours shivering in this cave, waiting for the morning light. I was too scared and too cold to sleep. I'd drift toward it and then jerk awake in the middle of strange dreams.

I dreamt a giant dragonfly hovered above the road by the truck. It lowered a basket of food—donuts, hot chocolate, french fries. It was so close, I could smell it, that deep-fried, sugary smell. But I couldn't reach it. In another dream, I chased the fox, which had Phoebe's face and Phoebe's happy laugh. But I couldn't catch her.

By 3 a.m., I'd burnt up most of my stockpile of firewood and I realized I would have to leave my cave to find more or I'd freeze. I might not freeze to death, but my temperature could drop enough that I'd get hypothermia and it would be hard to recover from that, out here, alone, in the dark, far away from help of any kind.

I stuck my head out and looked up and down the shore. I couldn't see much. In a stargazing book, I read that we lose a lot of our night vision just staring into a campfire. It takes about half an hour to get it back. I climbed out of the chill of the cave into the biting cold of the open air. I picked up my flashlight, dried it on my jacket and turned it on. Nothing. I gave it a shake and tried it again. Still nothing.

I closed my eyes and stood listening. The wind buffeted against my back, whistling like ghosts through the trees above. But I thought it was not quite as strong as it had been. The storm was dying out, passing over these woods, moving south. When I opened my eyes, I could see better. The debris of torn trees limbs littered the shore. Some of them might be dry and burnable.

Picking my way carefully over the rocks, my eyes gradually adjusting to the dark, I saw that the shape I'd seen moving by the water earlier was gone. That convinced me that it had been an animal. But strangely, out in the open I felt less afraid than I had been huddling in my cave with my ears plugged. It's better to face things, I thought. Better to be standing on my own two feet than crouching and waiting for something to pounce. Sometimes hiding from something makes it seem scarier.

I remembered a field day at my school two years ago. Carly and I had just bought hotdogs for fifty cents each. We were about to eat them when four older boys walked up to us. One said, "Give me that." We took off running and they chased us. We scooted under the bleachers on the edge of the field. But when they saw us, Carly, who is just as small as me, which means about eighty-five pounds soaking wet, stepped out and stood in front of them. I tried to pull her back and caught her by the sock. She kicked her foot away from me.

"If you want us to lend you some money, why don't you just say so?" she said.

The boys were as surprised as I was. They looked at each other with their mouths kind of hanging open, all their scariness suddenly gone. Carly was right, I saw. They just wanted to be able to buy hotdogs for themselves.

She dug in her pocket and pulled out the change she had left.

"What do you have, Francie?"

I stood up slowly, cautiously. When I was standing, the boys didn't seem so big anymore.

"Fifty cents," I said.

"Hand it over then," Carly said. "You owe us a dollar seventy-five." She handed it to one of them.

They were still gruff as they took the change and walked away, but one boy turned and said "Thanks" and his voice was soft.

There are hungry people living in our small town, hungry people who even go to our school. Mom told me that. It never really sank in before, how it would feel to be hungry and smell those hotdogs and not have enough money to buy one. I had never known what it was to be really hungry. Until now.

I found some branches that seemed brittle enough to burn and carried them back to my cave. Then I built up the fire and sat waiting for morning to come.

CHAPTER TWENTY-ONE

I don't think I slept. My mind wandered to those boys and the way their faces had softened, to Carly with one sock slipping down her skinny leg, to the smell of hotdogs and tangy yellow mustard. I was cold, colder than I could ever remember being. I slumped close to the fire. Gradually, the darkness seeped out of the sky, the wind dropped and a muffled calm lay over the creek like a light blanket.

Something moved in my peripheral vision. I gazed down the shore. Yes, something was definitely down there at the water's edge. About the size of a dog, it jogged toward me. Then I recognized the four black socks of the little fox. Her golden-red fur stood out against the pale colors of morning. She came within a few yards of my fire and then sat, her black eyes steady and calmly watching.

"Good morning, little fox," I called. "We made it through the night."

My voice didn't scare her. She just seemed curious. Maybe she wanted to warm herself by the fire. I wondered if she'd retrace her steps the way she'd come, back to where the truck was.

"I'm not following you this morning."

I pulled out my map. There was the creek I'd drawn in. With my pencil, I sketched my cave and the fire. I would likely never see this place again, but it had served me well; I had survived the night and I had found water. I drew in the fox sitting there observing me, her two black-socked front legs neatly side by side like a cat.

The road I needed to get to was a thick black line on my map, running south to the edge of the bush where I'd plunged in following the fox, and north to help, to Mom, to home. Did the road have a name? Ms. Fineday said that naming a place made it familiar. That's why when European settlers changed the names of so many places when they arrived here, Indigenous people continued to use their own names. I wanted to name this road, a private name only I would use, to make it familiar, a friend. In British Columbia, we had places with names like Desolation Sound and Deception Pass. The names told stories you could imagine just by hearing the name. But those stories weren't the kind I wanted.

The fox cocked her head. I imagined her listening to my thoughts, wanting to say something to me. I stared back at her.

"Okay," I said. "I'll name it after you. Red Fox Road."

I penciled it onto my map. Red Fox Road. It was perfect. It wasn't only about the fox. Our last name was Fox, too.

I looked out at the bubbling water of the creek where I'd found Dad's hat. I wrote *Hat Creek* on my map and drew in a little toque. Now my map of the land looked different in my hands. It took on the shape of a world I was getting to know. It gave me hope that I'd find my way in it.

More than anything, I wanted to cross the creek and look for Dad. I blew my whistle repeatedly, just in case this morning he'd hear it. But setting out from here to look for him was the worst idea. Chances were, I'd get truly lost. Dad knew where the truck was. He could be there right now. And thinking of that brought an edge of panic that I had to fight down.

To get back to the truck, I'd have to start from the spot where I'd come down to the creek, then take compass readings exactly opposite to the ones I'd followed to get here. In theory, that should take me back to the flag I'd left on the X of branches. From there, my challenge would really begin. How far east of the road had I strayed? What could I use to help me find it?

My best chance would probably be to stay east of it, hiking north. Then, when I thought I'd gone far enough, I'd turn and walk west. As long as I'd gone far north enough, I should cross the road at some point.

I looked at the map again to make sure I wasn't missing something. When I looked up, the little fox was gone.

Once the sun had risen high enough to filter through the trees and warm the air a little, I packed up my water and set out. But I kept looking backward, hoping I might see some sign of Dad. I pulled his warm Canada Post toque lower on my forehead against the cool breeze.

I found the tree overlooking the creek that I'd marked with my knife, took a compass reading, then breathed deeply and began walking. I could not get distracted. I could not make a mistake.

Wind-torn branches and fallen trees, their trunks split and

shattered, had transformed the forest and made walking more difficult than before. I counted off the minutes, straddling deadfall and fighting my way through tangles of branches. There was the stump where I'd found the ants. The thought of eating more made me shudder, so I kept on.

In a few more minutes, I was back where the red flag on the X should have been. I didn't recognize anything. No X, no flag, nothing familiar. I thought I'd attached the piece of cloth firmly to the branch, but it looked like the wind here had been even stronger than down by the creek. It must have blown the branches and the flag away.

Unless I was in the wrong spot. Unless somehow my compass readings had been wrong.

A knot of worry tightened my stomach. I checked the compass again. I was pointing to ten degrees, which should be the right reading. My eyes swept the landscape, searching for the spot of red. Pale orangey inner bark of torn trees stood out like fresh wounds; a tumble of greens and browns stretched out around me, but no red. A woodpecker tapped in a tree somewhere above me. I looked up and there it was—caught in a branch high overhead, the red scrap I'd cut from my precious backpack. I was so relieved, I laughed out loud.

"Thank you, woodpecker!"

It would have been nice to take the scrap with me. I could use it again to mark my way, or I could keep it and maybe try to sew it back into my pack if I . . .

I stopped myself. *When. When* I found my way back home. I took out my water bottle and had a swallow. I'd done well to get back to the flag. Now came the tricky part.

Logic said I couldn't miss it. If only I knew how long I'd followed the fox yesterday. I guessed it might be half an hour. Not as long as an hour, I was pretty sure. The worst thing would be to turn west too soon. If I did that, I could walk within yards of where the road petered out and not see it. Then I'd be in deeper trouble, wandering west into thick wilderness.

One hour, I decided. I would walk straight north for one hour. Then I'd make the turn west. Eventually, I should end up back on Red Fox Road. I would keep track of my time again and if worse came to worst, I could always find my way back to this point, the red flag in the tree. And try again.

The thought of that made a shudder run through my body. I could not bear another night out in the cold. I'd never had much meat on my bones, as people always liked to remind me for some reason, and that seemed to make me feel the cold more. The sleeping bags had been enough to keep me warm beside my fire, but without them, the cold had made it impossible to get comfortable enough to sleep. I could feel it this morning, the grit in my eyes, the raw throat. I needed to get to the safety of the truck and the protection of the sleeping bags.

One hour would probably take me too far north. But better too far than not far enough.

I had one last look at my red flag, feeling a strange mix of happiness and sadness, like a warm fist around my heart. This little bit of me, my most treasured possession, would flap here alone in the wind, maybe for years. No one would see it, except for birds and chipmunks, maybe a deer. But it would be here as the night fell, the moon soaked the woods, and the rain, then snows of winter came. *I was here*, it said, and no one heard.

"Wish me luck," I said to the woodpecker and began the walk north.

After five minutes, I checked the compass and looked for a landmark. Since it all looked the same, I took out my jackknife and carved an *F* on a tree. I didn't count on being able to find it again, but it was something. I kept it up, walking five-minute sections, sometimes carving another *F*, sometimes finding a fallen tree, a stump, a big rock, and marking these on my map.

The sun broke through the canopy of needles and leaves, spreading golden sprays of light through the branches. If I closed my eyes, I could picture where it came in the living room window, shining through the honeysuckle vine winding up wires that Mom had fastened to the window frames outside. I had held the ladder for her while she screwed in the eyes to guide the wire. Each spring we hauled out the ladder and strung a new wire for more honeysuckle vines to climb. In June, it would blaze with red-orange flowers like tiny trumpets and if I sat still in a chair by the window, I could watch the humming-birds dart from trumpet to trumpet and then disappear with a blur of wings.

In winter, the morning sun splashed in the side door of the kitchen. Mom liked to drag a chair there on weekends to read the newspaper and sip her tea in the pool of sunlight. She had a special china teacup and, when the sun shone on it, I could see through it.

Now, the sun made a reliable guide to help me keep on track without having to check my compass too often. After half an hour, I stopped and listened. I thought I might hear the engine noises I'd heard the other day. But all I heard were crows squawking and a chipmunk's chatter. Nothing looked any different than it had a few minutes ago. But I had to keep alert. Even a slight change in the shadows or the amount of light up ahead might give me a clue about where Red Fox Road was.

I stopped again twenty minutes later. Now I was pretty sure I was already walking parallel to the road. The truck probably sat a couple hundred yards or so to my left. I sat on a log in a patch of sunlight and took out my water. My gaze swept the woods, looking for something, anything familiar. And then I saw it. To my right, not far, was the rise of land. My eyes followed its length, then my heart sent up a spark. My fluorescent orange T-shirt blazed in the sun. I'd found it! I'd found my way back!

Excited but careful, afraid to make a mistake now, I clambered over logs and under fallen trees. The storm had cut a destructive path through here, ripping big trees up at their roots and exposing fresh black soil underneath, snapping others in half, leaving high, jagged stumps that would become homes for owls and woodpeckers.

When I reached my orange T-shirt, I ran my hands over it, closed my eyes and felt a wave of dizziness and then loneliness for my bedroom at home, the soft gray and pink quilts Mom had made for me and Phoebe when we were little. I'd kept mine, even though it was meant for a crib. I pulled open my dresser drawers and saw warm socks, fresh underwear, T-shirts I'd outgrown but still liked, corduroy pants and clean jeans. I saw the rocks I'd collected lined up on the windowsill, the glowing stars I'd stuck to the ceiling in the pattern of the Big

Dipper, and my bedside lamp, which had been Grandma's, and had a base like a log cabin and a switch on the bottom to turn on the lights at the cabin windows.

I hesitated, trying to decide whether to take the T-shirt with me or not. I could keep it where it was as a marker, but it might come in handy again. I untangled it from the branch and tied it to my pack. Then I skipped up the trail I knew well by now, passing the familiar rock.

But before I even reached the road, I felt that something was wrong.

I saw my lean-to through the trees and then, beside it, something new—the trunk of a fir tree lying horizontal way up in the air. A tree had blown over right next to the lean-to. The massive roots rose like a giant brown hand, with rocks caught between its fingers. As I came out onto the road, I saw where its trunk had landed.

CHAPTER TWENTY-TWO

Of all places.

Of all the possible places that a tree could fall in this forest, this one had to fall on our truck.

I stood staring at it, my mind not ready to believe what I was seeing.

It was a huge tree. That thought kept circling in my sloweddown brain. A tree lying down looks even bigger than a tree standing up. This one's trunk was limbless on the bottom part that had fallen across the east side of the road. Just about where it hit the truck, the limbs began. They were taller than me, fanned out in a dense green web high above the truck. Some pieces had snapped and landed on the hood and road. If trees had blood, that's the smell that hung in the air—raw, fresh resin, and ripped-open bark.

The roof of the truck was crushed nearly to its wheels. As I moved closer, I could see that the backseat and a corner of the toolbox had been flattened. The windshield had shattered but the dashboard was still recognizable. The note I'd left still sat there, barely visible under the web of branches. Limbs draped the hood. It had sprung open a crack, but hadn't been crushed. The rest of the tree continued across the road onto the west side and had gotten caught up in another tree's branches in the woods on the other side.

A single word formed in my head and I spoke it out loud. "Why?"

Then I screamed it at the top of my lungs.

Fear came rolling over me then like a billowing cloud of black smoke. My supplies—the sleeping bags, matches, stove fuel . . .

"Mom!" I cried out. "Mom! Where are you?"

I called her over and over and over, until my throat was raw.

A sputter of tears caught and died. The glass of the broken windshield glimmered in the sunlight. Trees tossed gently in the breeze.

I was doing it again. I was hoping for rescue—for Mom or Dad or both to come dropping down out of that helicopter, with hugs and kisses and warm blankets and a basket full of food.

Where was Fierce Francie?

I couldn't hear her voice, but I thought I knew what she would do.

What supplies could I save? What could I reach in the truck? I fought back the branches and tried the driver's door. It gave only a crack, as I'd guessed. There would be no way to get in the truck that way. If only I had the crowbar. But it was under the front seat.

No, it wasn't! I'd used it to make my drumming noise and I'd left it in the back. I climbed onto the truck bed and under the strong arms of the fallen fir. I could see it, but I couldn't reach it. There were too many boughs in the way. I'd have to try to break some of the branches, but they were big and supple and I couldn't do it by hand.

Eighty-five pounds is not enough to break live branches from their trunk, I discovered. I climbed to the edge of the truck bed and jumped down on the branches. They bent, but didn't break, except for a few twigs.

More likely to break was my ankle. I considered the toolbox, which lay twisted and bent under the weight of the fallen trunk. There might be something in there I could use to clear the windshield glass. It had popped open slightly on one end, but to try to get anything out of it would be to risk tearing my arm open on the sharp metal edge. But I might be able to get a branch in there. I jumped down and searched for a sturdy branch the right length.

When I found one, I climbed back up and found an opening in the toolbox to wedge the branch in. I wriggled it in farther and pressed down with both hands. The toolbox lid gave a little, but when I released the pressure, it caved back in. I tried again. Both hands and one knee pushed down like a big can opener. The lid rose, rose, rose and then—slam. The branch slipped, I fell backward, tree limbs scraped my back and the branch popped up, gouging my shin.

My body had sunk into the tangle of branches. I couldn't get up at first. I lay there a minute, catching my breath. Now that I was down there, I found I could almost reach the crowbar. Carefully, I reached my arm a little deeper under the limbs. My fingers touched the claw and closed around it. I pulled it toward me and untangled it from the web of branches. Then

I used it to help me push myself from the mess of boughs I'd landed in.

I climbed down from the truck gingerly. I'd have a big gash on my shin. My jacket wasn't ripped, but it was streaked with sticky resin, and the skin over the bony part of my spine stung from the scrapes.

My brain frothed like a pot of potatoes boiling over. Getting frantic would not help my situation. I had to calm down and think clearly. I had not allowed myself a cup of tea and a mint this morning; I'd been in too much of a hurry to find my way back to the truck. I needed to do that now. I only had four mints left and I'd been reluctant—no, afraid—to eat the last ones. What would happen when I ran out?

I got the stove out of my backpack and set it up. Then I squirted water into the pot from the bag I'd collected at the creek and put it on to boil. As I stared into the water, waiting for it to bubble, a few drops of rain speckled the surface. My work with the toolbox had kept me from noticing the sky had clouded over. The air had grown chilly, too. The icy rain made a hiss as it landed on the warm water. Then the hiss grew to a gentle peppering on the truck hood, the leaves and grass along the side of the road, and in a moment, big white snow crystals filled the air.

I shivered. My back hurt. As soon as the water rolled to a boil, I threw in a few fir needles and carried the pot to my lean-to. I had to be careful. With my luck, I'd trip and burn myself. It just seemed like everything that could go wrong had gone wrong. I tucked in under my lean-to and blew on the hot water. Fishing a mint out of my meager supply, I popped it in my mouth and sucked on it slowly.

The torn roots of the toppled tree lay only a few steps from my lean-to. Fast-falling snow sifted over it. I couldn't believe my bad luck. The safe place where I could have ridden out the storm lay smashed under a tree. No other trees had fallen on the road.

What would have happened if the wind had been blowing from a slightly different direction? If the roots had been weakened in one spot by a burrowing animal? If the roots had let go of their hold on the earth a moment sooner? A slight change in anything and my lean-to could have been crushed. I could have been in it.

My teeth chattered as I took a sip of tea. Each crystalline flake of snow landed on my jacket and melted. I knew I should start a fire before everything got too wet. A few dry twigs lay close at hand and I gathered these into a pile in my firepit. It occurred to me that I should have had all the kindling I would need with the fallen tree on our truck. But green wood doesn't burn easily, and it's especially useless to start a fire. I lit the match and held it to the twigs, watched it catch and gobble the kindling. I needed bigger branches for the fire, but that would mean getting up.

My shin had begun to throb where the branch had gouged it. Gingerly, I pulled up my pant leg to have a look. It was worse than I expected. A line of blood ran down my leg and into my sock. The wound itself looked like an animal bite, a ragged hole surrounded by red skin. I knew it would get more painful before it got better. I needed to make some kind of bandage to keep it clean. I needed to get warm. I just didn't want to do one more thing.

Sick and tired. That's what Mom said when she was really mad: *I'm sick and tired of this.* What did she mean by *this?* I never knew exactly. It could be whatever she was doing at the time: scrubbing dishes or angrily chopping potatoes, sending them skidding across the counter and onto the kitchen floor. Or sometimes she said it more gently, doing some ordinary thing like opening the mail, and that was worse. But now I thought I knew what she meant. Because right now I was *sick and tired.* I wanted to stop trying. I was cold and wet to the bone. I just wanted to stop.

The little fire I'd started struggled to burn. The kindling was mostly ash already, trailing a thin wisp of smoke. In another minute or two, it would sputter out altogether. Each flake of snow landed with a tinkle; those that landed on the ashes hissed as they died. A metallic taste filled my mouth, then a buzz filled my ears, traveled to my eyes, and everything went black.

"Francie?"

Phoebe. I struggled to open my eyes. Suddenly I was warmer, as if someone had wrapped a blanket around my shoulders. The soft smell of Phoebe surrounded me. Snow crystals tinkled and whispered softly. I could just let go. I could sleep here for a while and maybe someone would find me. I tasted the hot chocolate I'd drink then, the sweet heat of it traveling down my throat and into my stomach, warming my whole body. My pillow from home under my head, heat blowing from the vent under my desk, the stars on my ceiling glowing happily. In the morning the sun would shine through my bedroom window.

❖

Somewhere deep in my brain, another thought stirred: shivering. Something about shivering. Was I still shivering?

I needed to open my eyes.

Hear the snow falling? That's the real world.

A flake landed on my cheek and then another. I opened my eyes. A white sky with long green fingers reaching across it. Snow peppering my face. Yes, I was still shivering. I was shivering like a shrub in a stiff wind. But that was good. That's what my brain had dug up from somewhere in its memory: that one of the signs of hypothermia (that's basically on the way to freezing to death) is shivering. But an even worse sign, a sign of being too far gone to recover, is if you *stop* shivering.

My fire had died. Everything lay drenched under a crust of icy wet snow. I wanted warmth. My brain stubbornly wanted it to just appear, as it had when I closed my eyes. But that was not going to happen.

If it happened that way, I would die.

There was nothing else to do but force myself to stand up. I stomped my feet. My limbs felt heavy, like my boots were full of rocks. A sharp stinging sensation ran through my toes and heels. I jumped up and down and cartwheeled my arms a few times. Finding dry tinder or anything bigger to keep the fire going was going to be a problem now. Each needle on the tree boughs, the bark on the trunks, the dry grass along the road, the forest floor and fallen logs were coated in wet crystals. Even the lichen hung from the branches like the white beards of old men.

I gathered some of that and shook the ice out as much as I could. Then I stripped some branches whose needles had turned orange and I beat them against the fallen trunk to knock out the ice. The needles fell off, too, which I should have known they would do. I wasn't thinking clearly. I remembered that I had stashed some larger branches under the truck. Would it be possible to get to them? I had shoved them under the driver's door, in just about the worst place to try and get to them now. That's where the thickest branches of the fallen tree fanned out.

I gave up that idea and scraped the sticks I had into a pile around some lichen. I mentally crossed my fingers, then lit a match. The flame licked at the damp lichen and caught. The dead needles threw up a bright tongue of flame and then died. In a few seconds, the pile became a smoking, soggy mess. I tried again, my fingers shaking crazily. I dropped the match too soon and it went out. At this rate, the matches I had left would be used quickly.

One match. That's what Grandma taught me to do—light a fire with one match. The reason, she said, was not to be cheap with matches. Using only one match taught me to take time with the preparation. A good fire was all about the preparation. I knew that. But I was freezing and if I didn't get warm soon, I was pretty sure I'd be in big trouble.

All the more reason to take your time, Francie. One match. Get it right.

All right, all right. What could I use? I blew on my trembling red fingers, stood and stomped the blood back into my feet again.

Maybe I could get to that dry wood under the truck after all. I might be able to shimmy under the truck from the back. I walked to the rear, which hadn't been crushed by the tree, and I looked underneath. I'd have to get down on my stomach and elbows. It would be wet and muddy, possibly oily. I ducked under a little more to see if I could even reach any of the wood.

That's when I smelled gasoline.

I don't know how I didn't notice it before. Now that I did notice it, the smell seemed to fill the air. Obviously, gas was leaking out of the tank, which must have been damaged by the crash-landing of the tree.

My first thought was to wonder whether there was any danger of the gas igniting. My fire was far enough away that it seemed unlikely. My second thought burst into my brain like the spark of flame I so badly needed.

Gasoline would be a good fire starter! But how could I get it out of the tank? Could I find the leak and try to catch some of it? That would mean crawling under there and probably coating my clothes in gasoline, not a good idea. I'd seen Dad siphon gas from the truck when he needed to do a repair. He'd stuck a hose in through the fill hole, and then sucked on it to get the flow going.

"I don't recommend this method," he told me. "You have to be super-quick. I've ended up with a mouthful of gas more than once when I didn't pull the hose away fast enough."

I could probably use my jackknife to cut a piece of hose from somewhere in the engine. Then I'd need something to catch the gas in. I looked around, considering what I could use. But then I got a better idea.

I didn't need to put the gas in a container. All I needed to do was get some on a cloth. And to do that, I could just stick something down into the tank and pull it back up. The bonus to this idea was that I wouldn't have to take the chance of getting a mouthful of gas.

Beside the road, I found a bush that looked like a willow. I cut a long, flexible branch and stripped off the side twigs. I considered tying a piece of cloth from my backpack to it, and then I considered my fluorescent orange T-shirt. But I didn't want to use either of those and, also, I didn't think those types of fabric would absorb gasoline that well. I thought about cutting a piece of the hood off my hoodie, but the hood was good protection against the cold. So instead, I cut off one of the pockets. I pulled out the drawstring and wound it tightly around the fabric, fastening it to the willow branch. It looked almost like a wiener on a roasting stick, a thought that made my mind wander again to Carly and the field day and then to Carly's dad's barbecue, burgers and wieners lined up sizzling on the grill.

It took a few tries to get it to work. First, the fabric was too bulky to go in the fill hole. Then I broke my stick. After that, I lost the cloth down the hole and had to cut another, smaller piece from my other pocket. And I'd forgotten the tank was nearly empty. In the end, the cloth didn't get soaked; only a corner was dampened with gas. But that would be enough.

I poked the cloth, still on the stick, under the tinder and kindling. I didn't want to get too close to light it. The map was still on the dashboard, under a corner of cracked but not broken glass. I carefully reached my hand through the broken part of the windshield and pushed it along the dash until I could fish out the map. I tore off the southern third. I wouldn't need it now. Scrunching it into a ball, I pierced it with another long branch. Then I lit it.

With the long branch, I touched the ball of flaming map to the pile of kindling. Whoosh. It ignited in a burst. I jumped back.

Within minutes I had a hot, good-sized fire that wouldn't be drowned by the drizzly snow. The blood began to warm in my hands and feet. My shivering gradually calmed. I could breathe, I could think again.

A spot of color caught my eye. My first thought, crazy as it sounds, was Phoebe. Was I starting to lose my mind out here? She felt close somehow, as if she was with me. But it was the red fox, tiptoe-tiptoeing through the slush, with something hanging from her mouth.

"You're back," I said, and she stopped and stood watching me, her bright eyes intense, as if she were trying to tell me something. Her bushy tail nearly touched the ground.

"What is it? What do you want?"

She stepped closer and I saw that the thing hanging from her mouth was a frog, its legs dangling limply.

"Where did you get that?"

Could I eat a frog? Frogs were edible.

All frogs? I didn't know. My survival guide was in the truck, buried under a tree. But if the fox could eat it, I assumed I could, too.

She tiptoed softly away, melting back into the woods on the other side of the road. It seemed miraculous to me that a little creature like her could survive out here on her own.

If I could get over the fact that it was May and snowing, and my only protection was a lean-to made of sticks and a fire I'd had to light with gasoline, I could have better appreciated how beautiful it was. But it *was* beautiful anyway. Not just the little red fox. Not just the clear crystals landing softly on my knees, their intricate structures dissolving within seconds.

Not just the snow frosting the road and bush in sparkling ice. Something else poked through like the crocuses that poked through the snow in our garden in spring. It wasn't exactly happiness. It was just—warmth. My face was warming and a glow spread from a tiny spot deep in my chest. I was alive. And that was something.

I realized I'd been seeing this all wrong. I could have been in the truck. I *would* have been in the truck, huddling against the windstorm last night, if I hadn't been lost and holed up down by the creek. It wasn't bad luck at all. It was good luck. Amazing, incredible, stupendously stupid, wonderful good luck.

CHAPTER TWENTY-THREE

Dense brush, wet with rain, blocks my path. I fight through it, the branches pushing me back like the big waves that surge in on Okanagan Lake and knock me to my knees. Up ahead, beyond the bush, yellow lights pulse out of the darkness. I fight my way closer. A rain-slick highway shines in the flashing yellow light. Wet branches slap at my face and arms. The lights can't be more than a few steps away, but I can't seem to get any closer. I feel tears rising, clogging my breath. Then a movement shudders the brush. It's the little red fox, down low, picking a clear path through. I bend and follow her.

Out on the highway, the only vehicle is a tow truck, two flashing yellow lights on its roof. There's Dad, leaning against the side. Above the diesel rumble, I hear him.

"Hi, Squirt. You made it."

I can see the silhouette of Mom's head inside the truck. She doesn't turn to me, but I hear her voice.

"I told you not to leave the truck."

It was dark when I woke. My heart burned like a fresh bruise, beating in my fingertips and ears and throat and toes. The embers of the fire still glowed red but the flames had died.

The dream had been so real; the diesel smell still stung my nostrils. I tasted salt tears. I had not meant to fall asleep. It was dangerous, without my sleeping bag; the side I'd been lying on was stiff with cold. I drank some water, then rekindled the fire. In the firelight, I checked my watch. Only five after nine. Five after nine and I'd just slept about four hours. Maybe more. I'd be awake now most of the night, awake with the smashed truck, the black night, and the dream. I needed to do something.

In the glow from the fire, I climbed onto the hood of the truck and used the crowbar to clear the glass remaining in the windshield, fighting back the thoughts that pressed in on me like mosquitoes at the screen door of a tent.

Mom told me to stay with the truck because it's what she always told me. When we were little, when Phoebe was still alive, she told us that if we ever got lost, we should just stay put and wait for her to find us. Every once in a while, someone would go missing in the hills and mountains around our town. From our kitchen window, I could look across the back lane beyond the hydro wires lined with pigeons and magpies, past the shingled rooftops steaming in the sun, and I could see the mountains that rose up from the valley, the closer hills sage-dotted on the lower slopes, and behind that another range, furred with trees and snow-dusted in winter, and behind that, one more range, blue in the distance. Sometimes we heard helicopters and I watched them circling and hovering as they searched for a lost hiker or snowmobiler. I knew that the people who were found were usually the ones who stayed put.

When I had cleared the broken glass away, I reached into the cab of the truck and was able to grab hold of my sleeping bag. I could see that it was stuck under the steering wheel, which had been jammed nearly against the seat by the fallen tree. I dug my hands in and tried to tug it out, being careful to feel first for bits of glass that could have fallen in.

It took me about half an hour, but I finally pulled it free, only tearing it in one place. I couldn't reach Mom or Dad's bags, and since my flashlight wasn't working, I couldn't see to try to find anything else. But as I stood and shook out my sleeping bag, I noticed the radio. It didn't seem to be damaged. I reached down and turned it on.

Jumping down from the truck hood, I spread my sleeping bag in the lean-to. Then I went back to the truck. Except for a slight crumple near the windshield, the hood had escaped damage from the tree. The crumple had caused the hood to pop open, and that allowed me to pry it open further without having to reach the lever in the front.

"R.I.P."

Dad gave me that warning about the dangers of getting battery connections wrong. "Red is positive."

That's the order to follow, too. Put red on the positive post first, then black on the negative. I hoped there was enough juice left to get the radio working. I'd left the wrench next to the battery, and I was thankful for it now. But I didn't even have to wait until I tightened the bolts. The radio crackled to life as soon as I put on the black cable.

"This is Heartwood Hotel at KLCC, coming to you from Eugene, Oregon, wherever you are tonight, on your couch, in your car, or working the night shift."

I pulled out what was left of the Oregon road map and brought it over to my lean-to. A high clear voice was singing. The glow of the fire against my sleeping bag filled me for a moment with a rush of well-being. At least I had this. I would be warm tonight. I had this voice to keep me company. A voice from Eugene, Oregon, a town where people were driving their cars and waiting at stoplights and picking up groceries, eating snacks on their couches while they listened to the radio. I looked at the map. Eugene looked to be a long ways away, west, I thought, of where I was. The town of Bend was to the east.

Mom had said to stay. "Don't go anywhere." How many days had I been waiting for her?

I heard her voice:

"You didn't listen and look what's happened now."

Then Grandma's:

"Stop it, Del. You'll say something you'll regret."

We were in the boat, Grandma at the tiller of the outboard motor. Phoebe lay pale and quiet in Mom's lap, her eyelids flickering in the sunlight. Afternoon, and the lake had blown into a chop, waves slapping the hull of the little tin boat. When the spray hit Phoebe's face, her eyes fluttered open and Mom wiped her cheeks gently with her sleeve.

I knew it was serious. Fainting spells weren't unusual for Phoebe, but normally she'd sit up afterward, have a drink of Kool-Aid and a cookie. She'd be tired then for the rest of the day, but more or less herself.

"Why did I bring her out here?" Mom said.

Grandma didn't answer. She kept her eyes on the boat launch on the other side. Wind and water sprayed her face and arms. My arms and legs were bare and shivering. I hadn't had time to grab a jacket. But I wouldn't say anything.

Phoebe was the one who started to run. She was the one who shouted, "Bet you can't catch me."

I wouldn't say that either.

I saw her there on the lawn, her hair lifting in the breeze. She stopped and turned to me. The hummingbird whirred and flashed and I watched it dart from the porch feeder to a high branch. When I looked back, Phoebe was on the ground.

The order that everything happened became important to Mom later. Even when she no longer seemed angry, she asked me to tell her again and again.

I don't know exactly why Phoebe died. I know it had to do with her heart and it didn't happen right away. Each day she was in the hospital, I woke up in our bedroom at home with the sun coming through the maple outside our window, and I was excited for Mom to take us down to the beach so we could float on our backs in the lake if the waves weren't too big. Then I looked over at her untouched bed and remembered. Each day, the weather was nicer than the day before and I waited for her to come home. But that didn't happen. Instead, Carly and her mom took me with them to the beach, but they liked a different beach than the one we usually went to, so we went there. The sand was too hot to walk on and you could hear the traffic on the highway.

Mom was at the hospital all day and all night. She had forgotten about me. But she wouldn't like it if I told her that.

Dad was the one who came to me one night. Summer had passed. A north wind clattered through the maple and moaned at the window. I was still awake, listening. Some neighborhood cats yowled at each other and then a dog started to bark at them. Dad sat on my bed and said, "Phoebe's gone."

"Where? Without me?"

"No," Dad said. Then he didn't speak for a minute, but made strange choking sounds.

"No," he said again. "She's passed away. Phoebe is dead."

I cried into his shirt and Dad patted my back and said to get up, he'd make me some toast and honey. We went down to the kitchen. Everything of Phoebe was there: her handwriting on our little chalkboard and her pictures on the fridge.

"Do you want to ask me anything?" he said, as he put the plate in front of me and sat down.

"No," I said. I ate the toast and watched Dad watch me.

Then I said, "Is Mom mad at me?"

"Of course not. No." But the way he said it so fast, I didn't quite believe him.

Afterward, I guess I had thoughts that any twin sister would have if her sister had died. I guess some of them were pretty normal thoughts. I don't remember a lot of that.

The thoughts that stick with me? They're the ones I'm not proud of.

After the funeral, Grandma took me to Gem Lake. The leaves had turned yellow by then. A cold wind shivered across the surface of the water. Grandma kept me busy during the day, hiking the woods or taking the canoe out if it was calm. But at night I lay in bed and listened to her cleaning up the dirty dishes. Then the screen door creaked and slammed as she went out and I knew she was standing in the porch having her last cigarette of the day and looking at the moon on the lake. And then I couldn't hold it in anymore.

I cried, trying not to let her hear me. I didn't cry because Phoebe was gone, not really. I cried because Mom blamed me and I thought she'd sent me to Gem Lake because she didn't want me around and because I'd thought—this is the worst thought of all the ones I had—that maybe once Phoebe was gone, Mom would pay more attention to me. But that hadn't happened. Instead, it was the opposite. I cried because I couldn't change it.

What kind of sister has thoughts like that?

I put another branch on the fire and pulled the sleeping bag closer around my shoulders. A gentle rain had begun to fall. The soft voice on the radio said, "The Eugene Public Library will hold its annual book sale on Saturday, May 10. I know I'll be there. Like I need more books."

I wanted her to keep talking, to tell me about the normal things going on in her town. I wondered if she was drinking a cup of coffee, with her feet up on her desk. I pictured her peeling a juicy orange, setting the segments on a plate so she could eat them while the music played. I wanted an orange so bad.

"Here are a few songs that borrow from books. We'll start with something from 1969. Robert Plant and Jimmy Page were inspired by Tolkien's *Lord of the Rings* when they wrote this song."

You know the thoughts that you try to keep from coming to the surface? Basement thoughts, I call them. They live down there; I can sense them hiding in the dark. But you don't want to let them up into the light of day. If I feel them scratching at the door, I do something to try to chase them back down.

Like the time Carly and I went to Lydia's house after school one day. Her parents weren't home yet and we heard their dog whining and clawing at the basement door.

"That's Butch," Lydia said. "I can't let him out until my mom or dad gets home."

"Why not?"

"It's just a rule."

"Is he dangerous?"

"Not really. He's just a dog. You know."

The dog flung himself again and again at the door, scratching like he was crazed and letting out strangled half-barks, half-whines.

"Are you sure he's okay?" I asked.

"He wears a bark collar; that's why he sounds like that."

"What's a bark collar?" Carly asked.

"You know. It shocks him when he barks. To make him stop."

"Anyway," I said. "Mom said I had to clean my room before she gets home, so I better go."

Carly frowned at me. She knew I was making it up.

191

As I walked away from Lydia's house, I could still hear the dog at the door. I swore if I ever had a dog, I wouldn't make him wear a bark collar. I'd felt sorry for the dog. But also, I kept picturing what he was going to be like when the door was finally opened.

My basement thoughts are like that. They grow bigger and darker the longer I keep them down there.

The music rang out in the dark and filled the quiet. *The time has come to be gone.*

My thoughts whined at the door.

I made myself think of Gem Lake. Last time I saw Grandma, we'd paddled all the way to the other end of the lake. We'd had lunch on a blanket in the sand. Grandma smoked a cigarette and we named the shapes we saw in the clouds. Kingfishers flitted along the edge of the lake. Sun shone on the water. At the cabin now, the canoe lay flipped over on a wooden rack under the pines. A drift of leaves swept in on it. No one took it out anymore.

It was better to let the thoughts out. The longer I kept them locked away, the more ferocious they got.

In the quiet between songs, the rain tinkled on leaves, the forest peeped and rustled and sighed. I lay down under the lean-to and burrowed into my sleeping bag. Around midnight, the radio station faded out.

The cold woke me. I checked my watch: 3:04 a.m. Since being out here on this road, I'd discovered that three in the morning is the time when a fire stops throwing good heat, when my body can't get warm enough and it seems like the night and the cold will go on like that forever. It's colder at 4 a.m. But 4 a.m. is closer to morning and to hope. Three a.m. is caught smack between the midnight and the morning. Fears tumble around my ears, flaring like meteors; my heart roars. The soft pop of the fire sounds like stealthy footsteps on dry leaves.

The basement door gaped open. My heart had stopped beating; the night poured in.

I could die here and no one would care. Phoebe would have cared, but Phoebe was gone. The world would close over the place where I'd been.

The memory calls to me. That time we went to the Gulf Islands. Aunt Sissy was staying at a cabin belonging to one of the lawyers she worked with. It was right on the ocean. She'd invited us out for a week. I remember Phoebe seeming stronger then. We took two ferries and we'd stood out on the deck with the fresh wind rippling through our hair, and our arms outstretched like we could fly. We'd watched over the railing for whales and when we saw three black fins break the smooth ocean surface, we called excitedly to Mom. Then a man standing nearby said, "Those are just porpoises. Porpoises are much smaller than whales."

I turned to Phoebe and she made a funny, sour face, secretly meant for the man. I thought that even if they were just porpoises, they were beautiful the way they arced above the water and slid back under, like a sleek black curl. The rest of that trip, whenever someone pointed out something beautiful, Phoebe said, "They're just porpoises!"

We spent most of our time on the island playing on the beach in front of the cabin, digging for clams but mostly finding empty shells that shone like rainbows inside, and building canals in the wet sand. But one hot day when Aunt Sissy was away for the day, after lunch was done, Mom said, "Let's get out of here for a while."

She put a lawn chair, some towels, and a jug of water in the trunk, and the three of us drove out to a spit of soft white sand that stretched out and nearly joined a smaller island.

"Just like a tropical paradise," she said. "And no one else is here."

We could have wondered about why no one else was there on such a perfect day, but we were Interior people, as Mom said later. We didn't know about the sea.

She set up the lawn chair and sat reading her book, while Phoebe and I explored the beach, collecting shells that we were using to make the walls of a starfish kingdom for the dead star-fish we'd found.

Every once in a while Mom called out, "That's far enough. Come back here where I can see you."

After a while, Phoebe said, "Look at Mom." Her book had fallen onto the sand and her head had drooped so that it looked like she had no head, just a straw sunhat where it had been.

"Come on," Phoebe said. She took my hand and we ran out to the very edge of the sand where it touched the blue-green water, shining like a mirror. Out in the bay, a boy was putting up the sail of his boat and as he banged around, the hollow wooden sound of the hull and the flapping of his sail echoed across the water. The ocean lapped at our feet and the sand seemed to dissolve beneath our toes, melting away into seawater.

Phoebe and I stood on the shore watching the sailboat, laughing about Mom asleep with her hat over her face. The water had reached our ankles, although we hadn't moved. And then it washed in to our knees and we turned to see if Mom was looking, knowing she would be mad. The water out in the bay, which had been so smooth, was ruffled now and gurgling like a creek. Then it reached our hips, and Phoebe and I looked at each other and I saw the same sudden fear in her face that I felt in mine.

We turned to run as the water rushed in, closing around our bodies. It surged to our armpits just as Mom looked up, her hat tumbled to the sand, and she lurched out of her chair, running toward us. I felt my feet lift, no longer touching the bottom. I grabbed for Mom's outstretched hand, but where it had been, it was suddenly gone. Phoebe was gone, too, snatched up from beside me and onto Mom's hip.

It might have lasted seconds, it was probably only seconds, but those seconds are still so vivid. Reaching for her hand and the shock of finding nothing there. It was probably only seconds, too, before the boy on the sailboat had scooped me up by the strap of my bathing suit, the elastic dug into my skin, my stomach scraped against the wooden edge of his boat and I tumbled in among rope and rubber boots.

The things behind the door become bigger the more I go over them again and again in my head, and I'm certain I know that that empty space where her hand should have been meant she didn't love me. It was Phoebe she saved and Phoebe she loved. She loved Phoebe better.

"*Who?*" came the call of the owl. "*Whooo?*" The forest echoed with it.

I pushed out of my sleeping bag, opened it out and draped it like a cape over my shoulders. The rain had stopped. Out on the road, I threw my head back, taking in the starry night. So crisp and clear. A snowfall of stars, bluing up the darkness. Some stars seemed to grow briefly brighter, then their light dwindled, then they pulsed back to brightness again. Some of these stars, I knew, were already dead, but their light was just reaching me now.

There was the cloudy path of the Milky Way. Really, it was just one of the spiral arms of the Milky Way. Earth was part of that galaxy, too, made up of a hundred billion stars, and next door to us, Andromeda, with billions more stars. And the universe contained hundreds of billions of galaxies.

I leaned against the truck and felt it all spinning around me. All the dead and living stars, all the owls, ants, bears, foxes and deer, all the creatures in all these galaxies, billions of other beings. I was just one among them. No more or no less important, but just one among them.

Strange, but looking up into the swirl of stars, I felt—found. Freedom flooded my body.

My own path had been clear all along. I had to do the smart, sensible things it took to survive. And what I had to do was take Red Fox Road and walk north.

CHAPTER TWENTY-FOUR

I woke before the sun with my head full of calculations.

I had thought Mom might walk ten hours in a day. I would have about fourteen hours of daylight, from dawn to dusk. Allowing for rests, searching for food and making tea, and at least two hours to make my camp for the night, I thought I'd be able to walk eight hours a day. Maybe nine, if I felt strong. That seemed like a lot. It seemed unlikely. For one thing, I didn't feel strong. I was starving. Literally starving. I worried whether I'd actually be strong enough to walk it.

Well, it didn't matter. I had to try. It was going to be a beautiful day, too. The sun was just coloring the sky above the woods with a warm, pink glow. I stood up to make my fire. There was something lying on the log beside it. At first I thought it was a mushroom and my thoughts went to my survival book and the caution it had about eating any unknown mushrooms in the woods. But when I got closer, I saw that it was a frog. A dead frog. Its legs hung down across the log just like the frog that had been in the fox's mouth the day before. I swiveled my head, looking for her. Had she brought me this?

Was that possible? However it ended up here, it was a gift and I wouldn't hesitate to eat it.

I stoked up my fire and put on my tea water to heat. How to cook the frog?

Last fall, I'd gone to take the garbage out one Sunday afternoon and I saw across the back lane that Duncan's garage door was open.

"Come and look at what I've got," he called.

I was surprised to see a deer hanging from the rafters. Definitely dead.

"I got it a few days ago. Clean shot. P-p-p-perfect."

"Wow," I said. I didn't know what else to say.

"Wanna watch me butcher it?"

When he saw the look on my face, he said, "You could learn something."

Because I like learning anything about survival and because I liked hanging out with Duncan, I said, "Okay."

"Pull up a stool. I'm just sharpening my knife."

As he worked, he told me what he was doing.

"The worst of it, I did in the field. Taking the guts out, all of that. It's best to do it right away. And then I leave the guts for the coyotes. That's only fair."

"I don't know if I could do that."

"But you eat meat, don't you?"

"Yeah."

"I only eat the meat I kill myself now. Otherwise I'm vegetarian."

"You are?"

"Yeah."

"What do you eat?"

"L-l-lots of stuff. Vegetables. Obviously. Rice. Beans. Lots of people around the world don't eat meat. Some people say they don't believe in hunting, but they eat meat every day. Two or three times a day. They don't want to know where their food comes from. To me that's hypocritical."

I didn't say anything, so he added, "You know, when someone says they believe something but they do the opposite."

"I know what hypocritical means. I was just thinking."

"The worst," Duncan said, "are the people who say they just eat chicken. They should go to a chicken barn. See what a chicken's life is really like."

"You've been to one?"

"Worked in one a couple summers ago. That's what made me start to think. A wild deer has a pretty good life compared to that. And this one I got with one clean shot. Right through the lungs. Perfect."

"What do you do in the field?" I asked him.

"You make a fire. That's what I do. To warm up my hands. Then you have to cut out the anus. Do you know what that is?"

I rolled my eyes. "I guess I know what an anus is. How old do you think I am?"

He shrugged. "You have to get the stomach out without puncturing it. You don't want to puncture any of the organs. That spoils the meat."

Laying the frog on a rock now, I took out my jackknife, took a deep breath and made the first cut.

I didn't know what I was doing. I was just trying not to pierce any organs. And whether cleaning a deer was anything like cleaning a frog, I had no idea. It seemed to have a lot of organs. It seemed to be almost all organs. I used my knife to scrape them out as best I could. But I realized the only real meat was on the legs, a little on the front, more on the back. I took a pointed stick and skewered the frog with it, the way you'd skewer a hotdog. Hotdogs are made of animals, too, I told myself. Duncan would say I was being hypocritical to be squeamish about it. I had just never had to see how a hotdog was made.

While the frog cooked, I packed up my sleeping bag. The aroma of the cooking meat began to fill the air; like a switch had flipped, hunger pains tore through my body. I doubled over; my head swam. I thought I'd be sick, so I sank to the earth and lay there with the cool mud against my cheek and I tried to calm my breathing.

Strange that except for the first couple of days, the hunger had not hit me like this. But now, so close to eating something solid, I felt like I'd die if I had to wait another second. But I had to wait. I couldn't risk poisoning myself with undercooked frog when I'd come this far.

To take my mind off it, I considered my pack. Was there anything else from the truck I should try to salvage before I set out?

I ticked off the things I'd be carrying: water, matches, stove, the almost-empty fuel canister I'd had in my backpack, the pot, jackknife. That took care of my needs for eating. Rain jacket, hoodie, Dad's toque and Mom's sweater, my sleeping bag. That was for warmth. Even if I could have gotten the other sleeping bags from under the tangle of the fallen tree, I probably wouldn't have taken them. Another one would likely not fit into my pack, and tying it on top would make it too bulky. The tarp would have been handy, though. But it was hopelessly buried under the fir branches.

Actually, I thought, stretching my arms over my head to get out the kinks . . . I went to the back of the truck and stood pondering it. The sun at that moment peeked through the trees and streamed warm golden light on my shoulders. Actually, I thought again, hoisting myself up into the truck bed, it was true there was no way to get the whole tarp out, but I could cut a piece of it. It could be useful for a lot of things—covering my pack if it rained, sleeping on, catching water, attaching to the roof of my lean-to. I pushed aside the larger branches with my body, then cut into the tarp at one edge. When I was done, I had a piece about six feet by three feet. Perfect. Not too heavy or bulky, but big enough to serve some purpose. I folded it neatly and stuffed it into the bottom my pack.

Compass, paper, pencil, what was left of the Oregon map. Back at the fire, I sipped my tea with the sun warming me. I turned the frog on its spit. Its skin was crisping up and peeling off. I could eat it soon. Then, because I was so ravenous, I ate two mints. One left. I folded the crinkly package closed and tucked it into the pocket of my backpack. As I did, I felt again the certainty that it was the right time to leave.

The frog, when it was ready, tasted like you might expect a frog cooked over a fire to taste—smoky, slightly swampy, a bit like pond water and pinecones. But it revived me and I felt stronger. I silently thanked my little red fox, and then I was ready to leave.

I wrote a new note:

PLEASE HELP. I've been stranded on this road for eleven days. I'm walking north along the road back to the highway. P.S. I'm thirteen years old.

I put it in a corner of the windshield where a bit of glass was left to protect it from the elements. I thought of someone coming upon it: forest workers or hikers, hunters or Dad or Mom. I took it back out and wrote: *P.P.S. I'm okay, but hungry.*

It occurred to me that if a helicopter did come out searching, they would not get any clues if they saw the truck from the sky. So I took a few minutes to gather some of the fallen branches and I formed them into two giant arrows on the road, pointing north. The wind might blow them away eventually, but maybe they'd be there long enough to do some good.

I did one last walk around the truck. The hood still rested open a crack and the crowbar jutted out where I'd left it.

Something told me to take the crowbar. *It'll be heavy*, I thought. What would I need a crowbar for in the woods? I started to walk away. Then I glanced back at the truck once more.

Take the crowbar, said a voice in my head.

Okay, okay, I would take the crowbar. I ran back and grabbed it, wrapped my hoodie around it and shoved it in the side of my backpack. The extra weight tugged at my shoulders as I lifted my pack back on and cinched the waist strap. I could always abandon it on the road later.

As I picked my way carefully along the road, slightly off-balance with the bulk of my pack and aware of the throb of my injured shin, the truck tugged at me, like a long elastic band had been tied from my ankle to it, and the resistance against it pulled me backward.

The red Mazda had been my nest since I could remember, me in the back, my knees up, my view sideways as trees and hydro poles and vehicles flashed by, Mom and Dad in the front, Dad's big tanned hand on the gearshift in the middle and Mom's feet against the dashboard, her hand sometimes trailing out the window, the curls of her hair lifting in the breeze, one sometimes catching a draft that wound it in a tighter circle. When we were little, Phoebe sat sideways in the seat opposite me, reaching out her feet to mine as we tried to get our toes to touch.

The truck smelled of sunshine, old lunches, peanut butter and jelly sandwiches, apples left too long under the seat, the perfume scent of an air freshener from Midas Muffler that hung from the mirror for years and said "Trust the Midas touch." And exhaust. After a drive, the rubbery tang of it hung in our clothes and wafted from Phoebe's hair as we played on the floor in our room.

The sun rose higher; my body relaxed in its warmth, my muscles loosened. I watched my steps, made them deliberate and sure. I stopped to take off my rain jacket. In the sunshine, wisps of steam rose from the mud; the forest breathed a rich, warm scent of earth and sap, and my ears tuned to the Oregon jungle noises: distant birds singing and near ones cackling over nests, woodpeckers hammering at trees and ravens shouting orders.

When I began to walk again, the backward tug was gone. I breathed in fresh air. This mild, sunny day stretched out before me. But for now I just had this step then the next, finding the solid ground.

CHAPTER TWENTY-FIVE

Once the sense of being followed gets in your head, it's pretty much impossible to get it out. It came late in the day when I'd started counting steps to push myself to walk a little farther. The sun had dropped to just above the tree line and everything had softened in the rosy-orange glow of that time of day. But there was still lots of light left and I wanted to make the best of it.

I had reached the 460s or seventies in my count, aiming for one thousand, when the hairs at the back of my neck began to tingle with that sense that someone was following me.

I stopped and looked behind me. There was nothing but the long empty road, striped with long blue shadows. No rustlings of leaves, no breeze, but the longer I stood there looking, the stronger the feeling. I felt that whoever it was had stopped when I stopped and was standing, like me, silently watching and listening.

I bent to shift the weight on my back, then straightened and turned north again, walking a little faster now. I'd lost my count, so I started again at one. I was only at five when I noticed something I hadn't seen before on the road. In the soft mud, tracks ran alongside the path where I was walking. They belonged to an animal, not a human. They were a little bigger than my fist, and they showed the sharp marks of claws on the toe pads. Each toe had been imprinted clearly in the mud.

I crouched and touched one, the cool mud indentation fresh and damp beneath my fingers. I was no expert, but logic told me the wind and sun would set the print quickly, the way the mud pudding that Phoebe and I used to mix up crusted over if we didn't stir it. Last night's rain would have washed out anything from yesterday. These were new. Something had been walking along here, not very long ago. My gut told me the prints and the feeling of being followed had the same source.

What had I learned about animal tracks? If you could see the claw marks, that was a clue. That meant the tracks were either feline or canine. One walked with claws extended and the other kept them sheathed. Which was it? Either a cougar or bobcat, for instance, if feline, or a coyote or wolf, if canine.

The strange thing was that the tracks showed I was following this animal, not the other way around. So how could it be watching me? I tried to think of tracks I'd seen. These looked a lot like a dog or a coyote. And the more I thought about it, I was pretty sure that visible claw marks meant canine. Cats don't normally walk around with their claws out. If they're running, their claws will grip the ground, but not if they're just walking normally. You hear dogs' nails on a kitchen floor, for instance, but you don't hear a cat's.

This mattered to me because I didn't want the tracks to belong to a cougar. Mom always said we had to be more cautious of cougars than of bears, because cougars might stalk small prey, like children. That's why she had always made Phoebe and me walk between her and Dad when we hiked.

"Tail-end Charlie," Dad liked to say from the back. "I'll be the cougar lunch."

"That's what dads are for," Mom answered.

So if the tracks were canine, and I was almost sure now that they were, they belonged either to a fox (but they seemed too big for fox, especially my little red fox), a coyote (they seemed too big even for coyote), a wolf (were there wolves in these woods?), or maybe some other animal I didn't know about. Or they could be a dog, but what would a dog be doing out here?

I had planned to stop for the night at around seven o'clock, when there would still be enough daylight left to make camp and get a fire going. Now I wasn't so sure. If this animal was ahead of me, maybe it was better not to keep following it. On the other hand, if I stopped, I'd have to face the silence and the night coming on. Already a hush had dropped over the woods like a blanket closing over the day. The stillness echoed like the sound after a bell rings.

I shook each leg and each arm to try to flush out the willies. I was tired, I realized. Hunger gnawed at my insides. My stomach felt like a scraped-out bowl. I wanted to keep walking. What would be the worst that could happen? I'd have to huddle somewhere without a proper shelter. Even in the dark, I could always get a fire going, if only a small one.

I went on, trying to ignore the quiet, focusing on the soft rhythm of my own boots on the muddy road. I walked steadily, the tracks beside me in a clear line in the mud. Then they were gone. My mind had wandered. I checked my watch. I'd been walking nearly half an hour since I last checked, but it was as if I'd been in a dream and suddenly woken up. I couldn't remember anything about the ground I'd covered.

All I could remember was my dream of french fries with gravy and cheese—poutine—that Dad and I got from Jeffer's, the fry truck. I felt like I hadn't just pictured it; I was there, waiting in the warm sunshine with Dad and Jeffer's voices humming like bees and then watching as the grains of salt from the shaker rained down like stars falling, dusting the table. Sprinkling out pepper. Cradling the paper cup of hot crispy fries. I'd felt the comfort of returning to our warm truck, heard the ignition turn and the engine bubble to life. But I had not been able to put one of those fries in my mouth.

Now, I retraced my steps to find where the tracks had disappeared. I didn't have to go far. Only a minute or two back, the tracks had gone from the straight line they'd been following to a confusion of prints crossing over each other in circles in the mud. I tried to find where they'd gone next—into the woods or backward or where—but I couldn't see any tracks leading away from the circles. It was as if the animal had suddenly vanished.

I started walking again. The light had softened with evening coming on, but the air was warm, almost thick. I was really tired. It was time to stop. Just ten more minutes, I thought, checking my watch. I was too weary to count steps. When I thought I'd done enough, I checked my watch again. It had only been five minutes.

I began to look for a good place to spend the night. As I slowed my pace, the weariness washed over me again. This place, right here, would have to do. I didn't think I could go another step. I had to gather wood. I needed to build some sort of protection from the night.

My pack slid from my shoulders and landed heavily on the earth. A tall tree with drooping branches was the best I could do for shelter. I rummaged for the tarp and pulled it out, spreading it on the ground close to the trunk. I wanted to lie down right there, pull my sleeping bag over me. But I knew I needed to keep out the cold and damp better. The crowbar came in handy to break off some branches from nearby trees; these I interlaced, teepee-style, if a little haphazardly, around the trunk. It wasn't perfect, but right then it looked like the coziest place in the world.

I dragged more branches from the forest floor. The windstorm had left a broken mess of them that made my job easier. Pulling up a larger log for a seat, I carefully built my fire, held the single match to the tinder and felt the reward of watching the fingers of flame spread and lengthen.

The good warmth of the fire spread heat to my twitching, exhausted muscles. I couldn't wait to lie down, to stretch out and rest my back. But as much as I wanted to relax into the deep quiet of the falling evening, I couldn't. The feeling of being watched returned stronger than before.

What a quiet night. I lit my stove and put a pot of water on to boil. The flare of stove gas seemed to roar in the silence. Hot tea, the last mint, and then I'd sleep. I looked around me, into the deep gloomy woods. When I turned back, the stove exhaled a hiccup, then went silent. The flame had died. Thick, unnerving silence. My fuel canister had run out.

I tried to whistle the little tune that Dad whistled when he worked on his cars: "Whistle While You Work." But even that took too much effort, and besides, the sound of it in the silence felt lonely and eerie. Even the leaves and branches seemed to be holding their breath, so motionless, waiting and watching. The tea water was only lukewarm; I drank it slowly, ate the mint.

My eyelids drooped. The firelight glowed behind them. The forest breathed with me, softly in, softly out.

I snapped awake. There'd been a sound—sharp, near. Unless I dreamed it. The moon was up and the woods in the light of it lay ghostly pale and still. As I stirred the fire, the pop of embers echoed like gunshots.

There it was again—a single bark. It rang out, hanging in the air so strange and lonely and out of place. I slid the crowbar quietly from the backpack and stood up, straining to hear approaching footsteps. Could it be a wolf? Would a wolf attack a human? And do wolves bark like dogs? It sounded like a dog. That's what made it seem so out of place, I realized. It was like a dog I'd hear in my neighborhood in the summer, when I slept with my windows open.

I held the crowbar in front of my chest, with the claw-side down. What would I do with it? Should I try to climb a tree?

A tinkle of metal on metal came from the road, then the distinct sound of panting. Out of the moon shadows, a shape appeared. It stopped on the other side of my fire, sparkling eyes gazing at me. Then it sat, cocked its head and I saw the collar, and the glinting tags.

It wasn't a wolf. It was a dog. Just a regular dog. All my relief came rushing out in a breath. He looked friendly enough, sort of like a German shepherd, but with pointy ears flopped over and a fluffy tail.

"Hey, buddy," I said, and he galloped over to me, his tail wagging.

"What are you doing here? Where's your owner?"

The fur of his tail and legs was tangled with sticks and burrs and his tongue hung panting from his mouth. I found myself laughing, crazily, with the let-out tension.

"You scared me. You know that? What's your name?" I ruffled the long fur at his neck and ran my hand over his soft, velvety head.

"You want a drink, don't you? I'll give you a drink."

I squirted some water into the cooking pot for him. He lapped it up in about five seconds. I filled the pot again and he emptied that just as quickly, then sat back, his tail wagging.

"I don't have any food. I'm sorry. I wish I did."

I'm not a dog person. Mom says there are dog people and she's not one. I'm not one either. We've never had a dog in our family, and usually, I'm a little afraid of them, especially when they come running up to me and jump on my legs.

But as I sat by the fire pulling burrs from his fur, I'd never been so happy to see a dog. He seemed just as happy to see me. He kept twisting around and licking my hand. After a while, he settled down at my feet and I kept working on the burrs.

I checked his tags—that must have been the tinkling noise I'd heard just before I saw him. One tag was turquoise with a phone number and another number on it; the other was red and shaped like a heart and said "Rabies vaccinated" with another number underneath. His collar was well-worn leather. Wherever this dog came from, I guessed he was a long way from home. And somebody must be looking for him.

After a while, he fell asleep. I got out my sleeping bag and spread it in the little teepee I had made. Then I built up the fire.

I thought about making some kind of leash for him. I didn't want him to run away. But it seemed unfair to tie him up. He was probably trying to get home, just like I was. Besides, I had a feeling he'd stick around. As I crawled into my sleeping bag I called out, "Hey, Buddy."

He came to me, his tail thumping the ground.

"Can I call you Buddy? I don't know your real name."

He lay down at my feet, put his head on his paws and went back to sleep.

Stripes of silver moonlight streamed in between the branches crisscrossing over me and Buddy. My tired bones seemed to sink into my sleeping bag and right into the earth. I closed my eyes and heard Buddy breathing, heard the whisper of the forest settling in for the night.

Rest your weary bones. Rest your weary mind.

Grandma used to say that to me when she sat on my bed out at Gem Lake nights when it was still light out and the sound of people down on their docks tying up their boats echoed across the water. I hadn't thought of that for a long time.

I wasn't tired. I wasn't ready for bed at all, I told her.

Shh, she said. She rested her hand on my chest.

Rest your weary bones. Rest your weary mind.

CHAPTER TWENTY-SIX

When I woke up, Buddy was gone. My disappointment was like a punch in the stomach. I felt my lip tremble and a giant sadness ballooned up in my chest, caught hold of my throat and stuck there.

"He's just a dog," I said out loud. Then I yelled "Buddy!" as loud as I could.

He came bounding out of the woods, his bushy tail swinging.

"There you are! Do you want some water? Good boy. We're in this together, aren't we?"

When we set out walking, I felt stronger. The sleep had helped. Having Buddy to walk with helped even more. I checked my watch—already quarter to ten. Later than I wanted to be, but I could still get eight or nine hours of walking, with what I hoped would be a short detour to find more water.

The trouble with my mind is, it doesn't always do what I want it to do. I was on that road, my feet were moving, my eyes were scanning for signs of water, but my mind kept running off, like Buddy, always ahead or behind, scaring up old scents or chasing down something yet to come. It ran ahead to our house in Penticton, where the big maple shades the lawn and the honeysuckle climbs the trellis at the front window, and when the red trumpet flowers bloom, hummingbirds hover in mid-air, darting from flower to flower.

I ran up the front steps, tugged open the door; Mom and Dad jump up from where they've been sitting in the living room, anxious and waiting for me. Mom's been praying, even though she swore she'd never pray again, and Dad has bitten his fingernails to nothing. We all cry and hug standing there in the sunny living room.

But that was all wrong.

None of that made any sense. They knew where I was. It wasn't like I was the one who was lost. They wouldn't just be sitting around waiting for me.

My mind didn't want to think about what made sense. Where they could be. Why they hadn't come for me. I didn't want to think about it.

High above me, a jet left a trail of white across the blue sky. The road dipped and smoothed a little and I noticed the corrugated steel of a culvert jutting out into a ditch, surrounded by rocks.

"Buddy!" I gave my best whistle.

He came snuffing through the underbrush.

"Look at this. A culvert. What's a culvert for? To carry away water so it doesn't wash out the road." I checked the ditch on both sides; there wasn't water exactly, but it was damp, a little swampy on the west side. Once the snow melted in the higher mountains, this could be flowing with water.

"Let's walk down a bit and see what we can find."

I took out my orange T-shirt and tied it to a tree near the road. Then I took out my paper and pencil and marked the time and directions. We were walking west. It was easy walking; there were some stumps here that looked like they had been cut fairly recently. Buddy ran ahead and came back, ran ahead and came back. I decided to follow the stumps, which seemed to be in a pattern. If I had a bird's-eye view, I could probably tell what it was.

Quite a few small saplings had sprung up among the stumps, but I began to think I was following a path. Buddy hadn't come back for two or three minutes. I whistled, then listened, and in the quiet of the sun-speckled forest, I heard the clear sound of slurping. He'd found water.

"Buddy!" Running toward the sound, I broke into a clearing. A big stack of fresh-cut firewood was piled beside the creek. Sawdust powdered the ground. My heartbeat quickened. Someone was near, or had been, very recently. No footprints or tire tracks that I could see; but the mud was hard-packed and bare, as if there'd been vehicles and foot traffic. Maybe someone had camped here. But there was no sign of a firepit.

I dunked my water bottle in the shallow creek, listening intently. Water burbled softly over rocks. A few birds trilled in the trees. Buddy slurped and snuffled, shook his head, clinking his tags. Then he crossed the creek and waded through the underbrush on the other side.

The sun felt good, beating down on me there by the water. I dug out a purification tablet and dropped it in the bottle. Then I peeled off my socks, rolled up my pants and stretched my legs out in the stream. The cold, cold water soothed my tired feet and the smarting wound on my shin. I held my legs in the water until the cold made my head ache, and then I lay on the ground to let the sun warm me up again.

I woke at ten after three. Slow, stiff, stupid, I pushed myself up. Where was Buddy? Ten after three! I'd wasted most of the day. I doubt I'd covered more than a few miles. I had to get going. But this clearing. Would whoever'd been here be coming back? And where was Buddy? I couldn't believe he'd leave me behind.

"Buddy!" I called. And in an instant he burst through the brush in the same place where I'd seen him disappear. He ran to me and licked my hand, his wet tail swish-swashing the ground. Then he crossed the creek again and ducked in at the same place. That's when I realized he'd picked up a faint trail in the undergrowth that I never would have noticed on my own.

I shouldered my pack and hopped across the creek. The trail had grown in with willow and horsetail, but a trail had definitely been hacked through here at some point, maybe last spring. I had to push the young branches aside, but otherwise it was easy to follow.

Suddenly, I was through, and in front of me a white metal wall rose like a mirage. I was at the back of a big, boxy trailer. Two windows with grating faced the woods. Around the other side, a large cleared area spread in front of the trailer. There were metal steps up to a door.

"Hello!" I called. "Is anyone here?" There were no vehicles and no tire tracks in the mud. I climbed the steps and knocked anyway. "Hello? Anybody here?" Buddy skittered up the step beside me.

"What do you think?" The door had a grate over its window, too. I peered inside. "I can't see anybody."

I knew that when our next-door neighbors stored their trailer for the winter, they took the battery and gas canisters off and put them in their shed. I walked around the trailer, but I couldn't see any batteries or gas. This was a big trailer. It was possible they were inside somewhere. I couldn't see any way to reach the higher windows.

Then I remembered the crowbar.

I might have spent thirty seconds considering whether it was right to use my crowbar to break into somebody's trailer. I went back up the stairs and jimmied the claw under the latch that had been fastened with a padlock. Three tries and it snapped. I turned the door handle, but that was locked, too.

It took me a bit more finagling to pry the door open, but it finally gave. Inside felt cool, new and dusty-dry. The place was neat as a pin, clean and disappointingly empty. It was obviously meant as an office or headquarters, maybe for forest workers. A U-shaped desk took up one end of the space. Opposite the door, a small table with two chairs was pushed against the wall. Beside that was a small fridge, empty, the door ajar, and a microwave on a counter. I opened the cupboards above the counter—also empty. Behind me, on the opposite wall, was a sink and another counter. I tried the tap, but there was no water. The top cupboards held a set of plain white dishes, cups and glasses. When I opened the bottom cupboard—bingo! Two cans of pork and beans and an unopened bottle of soy sauce.

"Woo-hoo! Buddy! We hit the jackpot. Beans! We have beans!"

I did a quick search of the rest of the trailer. At the back end of it was a bathroom with a shower, a bedroom with a bare mattress on the bed, and an empty closet. I couldn't quite accept that there would be soy sauce, and no rice. No rice, no electricity, no water. It seemed like this place had barely been used, and then it had been shut up for the winter. Maybe they would be back in summer.

In a drawer, I found cutlery and a can opener, a box of matches, four tealights and a cheese grater. My fuel was gone, and I didn't want to bother trying to get a fire going, so I opened one can, then I opened the soy sauce and poured a few good dollops on the beans. I scooped some out on a plate for Buddy. He gobbled them, nosed the door open and ran back outside.

Salty, sweet, saucy and delicious—pork and beans had never tasted this good. As I sat at the table eating, I noticed the room had darkened. A few minutes later, I heard the pattering of rain on the roof. Except when I looked out, I saw that it wasn't rain; it was hail. Buddy came running and settled himself inside on the mat by the door. Within minutes, the mud clearing was covered in white pellets.

I heard the wind coming before it hit. Then a gust swept over us, tore the door open and slammed it against the outside wall. Buddy scrambled up and scurried over to me. I had broken the latch when I jimmied the door, so there was nothing to keep it closed. I tried to slam it closed, but the wind ripped it back open.

I had to tie it closed somehow, but there was nothing in the trailer I could use, nothing in my pack that would be long enough. I jammed a chair under the handle, but it wouldn't stay there. Ducking against the wind, I ran outside and searched the area behind the trailer for a rock. I found one about the size of a pineapple and I carried it back and put it outside the door, then pulled it in as close as possible so at least if the door flew open, it would knock against the rock and be stopped. It worked, sort of. But the door still banged open about four inches, then closed, then banged open again.

There had to be something I could use. I walked through the trailer again. In the bedroom, the window had blinds. The cords might be long enough to tie to something to hold the door closed.

The night came on fast and very dark. Lucky, I thought, to be inside and not out there with the wind howling down the road. I looked out but I saw nothing, no stars, no moon, not even the faint glow that would tell me where earth ended and sky began. What a night. I missed my fire. Inside was as black as outside.

I sat in a kitchen chair in the dark with my hand on Buddy's soft head. There was nothing to see, but I wanted to see that there was nothing to see. Wind tugged at the door I'd rigged with window cord. It was just the wind, I knew that, but I imagined long fingers reaching in to pry it open. Even Buddy was restless. Every few minutes, he trotted over and sniffed at the crack where the outside whistled in.

"What're you doing, Buddy? Can you stop that?" He came back to me each time, and each time I put my hand back on the soft velvety fur of his head.

The trailer was a better place to be; of course it was better on a night like this to be here rather than under a tree in the woods, and I tried to feel how lucky I was.

It was so dark and empty, though.

I got up and fumbled in the drawer for one of the tealight candles. I lit it and put it on a plate that I set on the table. Now I could see my own shadow dancing on the wall. Now I could see that, except for Buddy, I was alone.

CHAPTER TWENTY-SEVEN

I'm not going to tell about how long and dark and windy that night was or how I worried that a tree would topple and crush the trailer with me in it, how the door banged all night, how I burned all four candles, for nothing, only to see the flames bend and give and bend again with the force of the wind that somehow found its way inside the thin trailer walls, how I prayed and cried a little and called Buddy to sleep with me but he refused to jump up on the bed until I dragged the mattress to the floor and finally he stepped gently onto it and lay down beside me, how I hugged his matted, dusty fur and wished we were outside instead with the other forest creatures who were in it with us, taking cover from the unstoppable wind and the unending night.

But I have to tell about the stupid mistake I made.

Buddy's sharp bark woke me on the morning of the thirteenth day. He was scratching at the door to get out and I assumed he had to pee and he'd been trained to bark to be let out. I unfastened the cord, pushed aside the rock and he scrambled out and took off running.

"Buddy, wait! Wait for me! Where are you going?"

I took a few seconds, ten or twenty, to think about what to do—stop and pack my stuff or follow him right away—and in those few seconds, I made the decision to follow him. I knew how to get back to the trailer, and he was after something that my gut told me I should go after, too.

I ran back along the little path through the underbrush, came out at the creek and hopped over it. I couldn't see him, but the jangle of his tags kept me on his trail, and anyway, somehow I knew he was headed back to the road. The stumps, coming on them from this direction, were easier to follow. I ran, with this growing feeling in my gut. Maybe my ears had picked up the sound Buddy's had picked up minutes earlier, but my brain hadn't quite made sense of it yet.

And then it did. And I knew a vehicle was coming down the road. From which direction, I didn't know.

I put it into overdrive, as Carly would say, and went as all-out as my muscles would let me. I burst out of the bush and onto the road just in time to see a vehicle, black, rattling away from me, heading north, with Buddy in a full-out gallop after it.

I screamed myself hoarse, flailing my arms like an idiot, long, long after it would have done any good. To be honest, it wouldn't have done any good from the start and I knew it. Buddy ran for a long time, too, good old dog.

I sat in the dirt and waited for him to come back and eventually he did. As I waited, I saw the T-shirt flag I'd tied in a tree. Stupid mistake. The only thing that flag was good for was marking the spot where I'd gone into the woods. Anyone passing by on the road would have to be going very slowly and watching very carefully to have seen it. I should have made some arrows with tree boughs, or dragged a fallen tree across the road or something, something, to stop a vehicle, to make them get out and wonder, and then I should have left a note, I should have stayed on the road, I should have never left it, I should have stuck to my plan to be where I said I'd be, to be somewhere I could be found.

I was so angry with myself, I sat on the road storming inside, kicking the dirt and yelling "stupid, stupid, stupid" for too long, willing the black vehicle to turn around and come back. When it didn't and it still didn't and it still didn't, I went back to the trailer to get my pack and the second can of beans. This time, I didn't leave the road without first dragging some big branches across it. I hung my T-shirt flag in the middle of them. I didn't have my pencil with me, so I couldn't write a note, but I took the time to gather a few rocks and spell out SOS with them.

Back at the trailer, I threw my things into my pack, scribbled a note of apology for breaking the door and taking the beans, included our phone number so they could contact us to pay for it, and ran back to the road. With each footfall, the words *stupid, stupid, stupid* rang in my head. Buddy panted along beside me as if he understood everything. That Mom or Dad or both could have been in that vehicle, passed once or twice, went on to look somewhere else, that I was supposed to stay with the truck, that Mom had told me to stay with the truck, that the note I'd left said I'd be walking north along the road and I was not walking north along the road or anywhere along the road. That if I was not where I said I'd be, I was like a needle in a haystack in this wilderness. I would be impossible to find.

When we got back to the road, I looked up it and down it. My mind was all in a froth, as Grandma used to say. It was a true disaster, the biggest disaster of my life.

Well, the second biggest. At least the second biggest. The first was chasing Phoebe that last day we spent together at Gem Lake. All through the years I'd told myself she was the one who said, "Bet you can't catch me." That was true. But there was more to the story.

We'd been in the woods. We'd been playing hide-and-seek in among the trees. We had a rule about no running, just to make it fair for Phoebe, who wasn't allowed to run because of her heart. But I'd dashed from one spot to another when Phoebe was getting warm, and she'd seen me.

"You're it!" she called out. She caught up to me and touched my shoulder. "You cheated. Running isn't allowed." Her face wore the look it sometimes got when she was trying to think of something mean to say.

"You've got skinny legs," she said.

"I do not."

"Yes, you do. I don't know how they hold you up. I don't know how you can even walk, let alone run."

"You can't run at all," I said.

"I can run. I bet I'm faster than you."

"You've got a hole in your heart and probably in your head, too. You're like the Grinch."

"He doesn't have a hole in his heart. His heart is two sizes too small."

"Same thing."

"I dare you," she said.

"You're not allowed."

"I'm faster than you. Watch me."

"Mom will be mad."

"You're it."

I didn't know what game we were playing anymore. But I gave her a head start and then I chased her.

She was right. She was fast. I never told her that, either.

I stood on the road shivering a little, because the day was one of those that are warm and cold at the same time—warm sunshine, nippy air. I felt full to bursting with the disaster it was that I had missed the only vehicle to come down this road in thirteen days. There was nothing I could do. Nothing at all. Absolutely nothing.

Okay, there was one thing.

I could make a fire. Right there in the middle of the road. It was probably useless, it was probably pointless, it was probably a waste of time. But I couldn't stand the idea of doing nothing.

So I gathered dead brush and piled it high in the middle of the road where it wouldn't spread to the woods, topped the pile with green branches and lit it. Before long, big billows of gray smoke rose tumbling into the sky.

I put on my pack and followed Buddy, who had decided it was time to start walking up the road again. I tried to keep up my brisk pace, as Dad called it, and it was almost two hours before the adrenaline that had been fueling me sputtered out and I realized how hungry I was. I hadn't eaten since the beans the night before.

I dug out the beans I'd taken from the trailer. Buddy had run some distance ahead, but he came back and lay near me, his turned-over ears twitching as he watched me. The deciduous trees here had not yet leafed out, though they were about to. The new buds lined along the branches made a lacy pattern at the edges of the road. But where the truck had broken down, the leaves were already out. That must mean we'd walked to a higher elevation, though I hadn't noticed.

Suddenly, Buddy's ears pricked up. He scrambled to his feet and stood listening. His ears turned this way and that, and he took off running, full tilt up the road.

I swallowed and strained my ears, but they only picked up the jangle of Buddy's tags and a high, shushing wind rippling through the treetops.

He'd got so far ahead of me already, there was no point trying to run after him. So I took out my jackknife and opened the can of beans. Then I scooped out a few mouthfuls, saving some for him, took a couple swallows of water and stuffed everything back in my pack. It was hard to run with the backpack on and a belly full of undigested beans. I only tried for a few minutes before I got a stitch in my side and had to slow down.

I could see him, way, way ahead, a dark dot on the muddy road. But after a while, I couldn't be sure that I really was seeing him. He'd gone on without me and I had to take deep gulps of air to stop myself from crying.

After a long time, as it became harder and harder not to

cry, I did hear something, a faint buzz like—I don't know what—like mosquitoes only bigger. And when my brain was on the brink of knowing what it was, it faded away and left me to the crows and the high moaning wind.

I tried not to notice how my feet hurt today and how my shoulders ached from the tug of the pack. With my eyes scanning the road ahead, I nearly stepped on a flock of blue butterflies fluttering in the mud. There were twelve of them, the most beautiful blue I'd ever seen. The bright blue, shining like the rainbow that oil makes in a puddle, was so strange and out of place, I felt I might be dreaming them. And maybe this empty road was a dream, too, and I would wake up in my own bed and hear our neighbor's country music radio floating in my window, mixed with the buzz of distant lawnmowers.

A soft wind rose and lifted my hair. Then a door swung open in my brain and the distant buzzing sound sailed in on the breeze, louder now, distinct. A lawnmower. It sounded like a lawnmower.

"Buddy!" I cried out. "Bu—ddy!" I thought I could see him way down the road, a dot getting bigger.

I ran and called, ran and called. I heard his tags jangle as he got closer. Then he was back, jumping on my legs and licking my hands, one then the other. His tongue hung loose and lolling, foam around his mouth. I got out my little pot and poured some water in it for him, which he slurped up in his usual vacuum-cleaner way. But immediately he trotted off again, this time more slowly, waiting up for me.

The lawnmower sound grew and faded, grew and faded, then grew steadily louder and another dot appeared on the horizon. As it drew closer, I understood that it was not a lawn-mower, but a dirt bike.

My heart thundering in my chest, I waved my arms crazily over my head.

The bike came closer and closer, then skidded to a stop a few feet in front of me. Buddy bounded over to the rider, who was dressed in orange and white leather, a black helmet that mostly covered the face like a mask, and knee-high black boots. My exhausted mind was playing tricks on me, and I blinked to clear the image of the fox, standing in front of me with her neat black socks. Then the driver pulled the helmet off and her long red ponytail flopped out. She bent to Buddy whose tail was wagging so hard I thought it would knock him over.

The girl stood up. "What are you doing with my dog? What are you doing way out here?"

"I'm Francie Fox. Are you looking for me?"

"I was looking for Buddy." She bent to him again and kissed his head. "You found him."

"He found me."

"Were you lost?"

"Not really. Your dog's name is Buddy?"

"Yeah. This is Buddy. He took off chasing a squirrel and he's been missing for four days."

"Isn't there a search?"

"Just us. Me and my dad. He's in his truck."

"Are my mom and dad out on the highway? We got stuck out here. Isn't there a search?"

"I don't know about any of that. I was just looking for my

dog. But I can take you out to the highway. I don't know about that backpack, though. It'll put us off-balance."

"I could leave it, I guess. Do you think someone could come back for it?"

"I'll ask my dad. He's with the truck near the highway."

"Is it black?"

"How do you know that?"

"You drove out this way this morning."

"Yeah, we did. Dad said I could give it one more try on the bike. But Buddy found me instead. He's a smart dog, aren't you, Bud?"

The girl took my pack from me and put it down by the side of the road. "We'll leave it here where we can see it when we come back. Don't worry. I'm sure Dad'll come and get it for you. How long have you been out here anyway?"

"Thirteen days."

"Thirteen days? Are you sure?"

I turned to the forest, where soft fir fronds glistened with sunlight. They stirred in the breeze like hands waving goodbye.

I climbed on the back of the dirt bike. There were no flashing lights, no helicopters or news reporters. No baskets of food and Mom and Dad running with their arms open. Just this red-haired girl on a dirt bike looking for her dog.

"Grab hold of me around my waist. Hold on good and tight. It's a bumpy ride, but we'll take it easy so Buddy can keep up."

She shifted to look at me. "Are you okay?"

"Yeah," I said. "I'm okay."

CHAPTER TWENTY-EIGHT

A steady beeping sound came to my ears. The bird, I thought. The road. An unfamiliar smell floated in the air—bleach and soap and food smells. And the air, too, was wrong. Heated, heavy, dry.

I opened my eyes on a white room, venetian blinds at a window, a blue sky outside it. It took a few moments to realize I was in a hospital room. A tube stuck into my arm was attached to a machine that drip-dripped clear liquid.

My mouth was so dry. I pushed myself up and saw a pitcher of water on a table beside my bed. With my free arm, I reached for it and poured myself a glass of water. Ice cubes tumbled into the glass. It was so sweet and cool. I poured myself another, then another. A nurse stood beside a counter outside my room. The tube was long enough to let me stand up. But when I tried, my legs gave out under me like plastic straws. I stumbled against the machine beside the bed and the clatter made the nurse turn.

"You're up!" she said, smiling. "Look at you! I bet you'd like some breakfast."

"Where are my mom and dad?"

"Your Aunt Cecilia is here. She just went for coffee. She didn't want to wake you up."

"But my mom and dad?"

"I'll find your aunt. She'll be so excited to see you're up."

Aunt Sissy, when she saw me sitting on the side of the bed, took me in her arms and squeezed me so long and so hard I could barely breathe.

"Your mom is here," she said. "Someone found her by the side of the road. She's not awake yet."

"Is she okay?"

"Yes, she will be. She's not hurt. The sheriff is here. He wants to ask you some questions. They didn't even know you and your mom were related until I got here. I got the call a girl and her father had found you walking along some remote road. You gave them my name and number."

"I don't remember that. I remember getting on a dirt bike."

"They brought you straight here. They couldn't tell me much more. They brought your backpack." She gestured to where it leaned against the wall. "All I knew to tell them was that you were on your way home from a trip to the Grand Canyon."

"No," I said.

"What do you mean no?"

"We never got to the Grand Canyon. We were on our way down. The truck broke down on that road."

"What road?"

"The road the fox-girl and Buddy found me on."

Aunt Sissy lifted my legs back up into the bed and pulled the covers up.

"Maybe we shouldn't rush things. You need to get more rest."

"No, Aunt Sissy, I'm fine. I mean, I feel okay. We never got to the Grand Canyon. We took a shortcut and then the truck broke down. Where's Dad? Have they found Dad?"

"But Francie, that can't be right. You left home two weeks ago."

"Have they found Dad?"

"No, not yet. Like I said, the sheriff needs to ask you questions. They'll do everything they can."

"I want to see Mom."

"The sheriff wants to see you first. He'll be up right away. He's getting coffee."

"I want to see her."

"It's just the way they do it, Francie. He'll talk to you and then we'll go see her."

She squeezed me again. "I'm so, so glad to see you."

"Can they take this thing out of my arm?"

The sheriff said the Canada Post toque was a good clue. He sat in a chair by my hospital bed with his Stetson hat in his lap. He wore the star badge like I'd seen on TV.

I showed him my map, which had been stuffed in my jacket pocket and was creased and smudged with grime. I had marked in Hat Creek and drawn the little toque in the spot where I'd found it.

"That's smart," the sheriff said. "This'll give the searchers a much better idea of where to look."

"I don't know if he dropped it on his way to find the highway or on his way back to us," I said.

"Good thinking. This map is really helpful. I've got a map to show you, too."

He pulled it from inside his jacket and unfolded it on his knees. "This is a topographic map. The lines show the elevation. Here it's higher, see? The lines are closer together." He put his finger on a line that ended in an expanse of milky green.

"Here's where we found your truck. I want you to show me where your dad was walking to. And tell me everything he said."

I looked at the map. The milky green was spidered with brown elevation lines and the blue of the creek running like a vein through it. But there was no road. A sick feeling rose in my stomach.

"I don't see it. He walked this way. There was supposed to be a road. Fifteen miles, he said."

"Okay," said the sheriff. He folded up the map and put it away. "Tell me about the weather the day he left."

I explained to him what the weather had been like over the days we waited for him. I watched his face, his slow nod. He wrote down the dates and times. Then he asked about the equipment he was carrying and I told him about the tent. The tent but no sleeping bag.

"If he set up the tent, that'll make him easier to spot," the sheriff said.

"Will you use a helicopter?"

"Yes. We have a helicopter. We'll use all the resources we have."

❖

The room Mom lay in was hushed and dim, the blinds half-closed against the bright day outside. Aunt Sissy opened them and sunlight poured in.

Mom's hair spread like a wild halo around her head on the pillow. A machine beside her beeped as steadily and rhythmically as the bird in the woods. I took her hand. It felt soft and warm, the very best thing I'd ever touched.

"Mom," I whispered.

"She's sleeping, sweetie," Aunt Sissy said gently. "I didn't even know she was here until I got here last night. Someone found her on the side of the highway. She was unconscious. The sheriff couldn't figure out who she was or where she'd come from."

"Mom, I'm here," I whispered again. "We made it."

I thought her eyelids flickered; I thought I saw a smile start on her lips.

Her lips moved. She was trying to say something. Aunt Sissy and I watched her. Her head turned one way and then the other. Then she whispered, "I came back for you."

"She's a little confused," Aunt Sissy said.

"You waited. And I came back for you," she said again.

"She's confused," Aunt Sissy said again, patting me on the back.

"I know," I said.

❖

That night I tried to sleep. A hospital is not as quiet as you'd think. Aunt Sissy was snoring lightly in a chair near my bed. Some machine was clanging on a floor above me. I heard sirens outside. Beeps and clacking wheels and unfamiliar rushes of noise filled the dark. I put my mind back in the forest, with moonlight streaming through the trees.

I knew that Dad would not have set up the tent. I knew he would have kept walking. Walking was what he did best. He may have sat and rested, or he may have fallen asleep as he rested. But I knew he would not stop walking until he couldn't walk anymore.

I pictured him walking through the rain, whistling. He stops for a drink beside Hat Creek, tempted by the clear, cold water. He's sweating a bit, so he takes off his toque, lays it down on a rock. Then he feels the clouds break. He lifts his head and looks up at the sky. The sun beams down on his face, and on the forest, making everything steam and shine. He stands and smiles, takes another step and keeps walking.

Mom had not come back for me. Not really. But she had tried.

And that, I decided, was just as good.

ACKNOWLEDGEMENTS

One sunny Sunday when my son was about Francie Fox's age, he, my husband, David, and I went off-road driving in our old red Madza on the backroads in the hills near our town. Having fun, we took increasingly rough roads, over rocks and across gullies, exploring an area we'd never traveled in before. As the day turned to afternoon, we tried to find our way out of the maze we'd followed, but we kept looping back to the same impassable spot. Hours later, low on gas and hungry, we finally came to a locked gate. David walked out and, luckily, found the farmer who had the key to the gate. We were embarrassed and a little shaken as he unlocked it to let us drive out to find the main road.

That experience stayed with me. I realized we had not paid attention to where we were going because we were only a few miles from home. Since that time, I've read many stories of people who've become stranded by following the wrong roads, sometimes suggested by their GPS devices. In 2011, a woman from our town survived forty-nine days after following GPS directions down a remote road in Nevada. Her remarkable courage also stayed with me.

While researching this book, I took a trip to Oregon. On my way back to Canada, I took a wrong turn out of a gas station and ended up about an hour east of where I should have been. That error gave me the idea for the Foxes' error in the book.

I'd like to thank Jenny Lippert, forest botanist at the US Forest Service, for answering my questions about the forest in parts of Oregon. Any inaccuracies that remain are due to my fictionalization of the landscape. Thanks to Henry at Midas for advice on engine troubles. I would like to acknowledge the profoundly peaceful writing time provided by Dorland Mountain Arts Colony, Playa Residency and the Saskatchewan Writers' Guild. I'd also like to acknowledge the support of Okanagan College, as well as Deborah Cutt, Surandar Dasanjh and Eva Gavaris at the Penticton campus library.

I thank my friends in adventure, Nancy and Glenn Noble-Hearle and Mary Kiviste, for helping me put to the test my theoretical knowledge about the outdoors. Dan Joyce, my father-in-law, is my living encyclopedia of knowledge about life lived close to nature on Canada's west coast. Thanks to Barbara Johnston and Jay, Anna and Sophia Draper for sharing their reading lists with me. Randy Lundy and Diane Zoell have shared their love of the natural world with me in many ways. Deepest gratitude to Denise Bukowski, who has been my tireless champion from the beginning. I thank my editor at Penguin Random House Canada Young Readers, Lynne Missen, for her whole-hearted belief in Francie Fox's story.

Love and gratitude to my siblings, Anne, Mary, Pat, Barbie

and Neil, for their support, and to my son, Khal Joyce, for all the things he teaches me. As always, deepest love and gratitude to my first and most eager reader and partner in all things, David Joyce.